D0770803

Emma's

Amish Faith Tested

THE AMISH WOMEN OF
LAWRENCE COUNTY SERIES - BOOK 1

Tracy Fredrychowski

ISBN 978-1-7342411-9-8 (paperback)

ISBN 978-1-7342411-8-1 (digital)

All Bible verses are taken from King James Version (KJV)

Published in South Carolina by The Tracer Group, LLC

https://tracyfredrychowski.com

8 For by grace are ye saved through faith; and that not of yourselves: it is the gift of God:

9 Not of works, lest any man should boast.

Ephesians 2:8-9 (KJV)

By Tracy Fredrychowski

AMISH OF LAWRENCE COUNTY SERIES
Secrets of Willow Springs – Book 1
Secrets of Willow Springs – Book 2
Secrets of Willow Springs – Book 3

APPLE BLOSSOM INN SERIES
Love Blooms at the Apple Blossom Inn

NOVELLA'S
The Amish Women of Lawrence County
An Amish Gift Worth Waiting For

THE AMISH WOMEN OF LAWRENCE COUNTY
Emma's Amish Faith Tested – Book 1

www.tracyfredrychowski.com

Contents

ABOUT THIS STORY...

While this story and its characters are figments of my imagination, Jesus Christ is very much the truth.

Throughout the United States and Canada, there are many conservative Amish orders that practice salvation through works. They believe only God can decide their eternal destiny by how well they stayed in obedience to the rules of the *Ordnung.*

Many Amish communities share traditional beliefs, much like today's Christians. However, some think the assurance of eternal salvation to be prideful and refuse to accept the truth as written in God's Word.

As I researched this story, I found more and more Amish communities are moving away from their old ways. It was heart-warming to discover the truth was being taught, and they have assurance in salvation through Jesus Christ alone.

Please keep in mind, not all Amish Orders are the same. And while I write the truth about finding salvation in Christ, what is practiced among the Amish may differ from community to community across the country.

A NOTE ABOUT AMISH VOCABULARY

The language the Amish speak is called Pennsylvania Dutch and is usually spoken rather than written. The spelling of commonly used words varies from community to community throughout the United States and Canada. Even as I researched this book, some words' spelling changed within the same Amish community that inspired this story. In one case, spellings were debated between family members. Some of the terms may have slightly different spellings. Still, all come from my interactions with the Amish settlement near where I was raised in northwestern Pennsylvania.

While this book was modeled upon a small community in Lawrence County, this is a work of fiction. The names and characters are products of my imagination. They do not resemble any person, living or dead, or actual events in that community.

LIST OF CHARACTERS

Emma Yoder. A young Amish woman and Samuel's wife.

Samuel Yoder. Childhood sweetheart and husband to Emma.

Katie Miller Emma's best friend and Samuel's sister.

Daniel Miller. Emma's biological brother and Katie's husband.

Bishop Weaver. A church leader in Willow Springs.

Marie Bouteright. Daniel and Emma's biological mother.

Levi and Ruth Yoder. Samuel and Katie's parents.

Lillian Shetler. Emma's biological Amish grandmother from Sugarcreek.

Jacob Byler. Emma's Amish father.

Rebecca and Anna Byler. Emma's older twin sisters.

Alvin and Lynette Miller. A Mennonite couple who ministers to young people.

MAP OF WILLOW SPRINGS

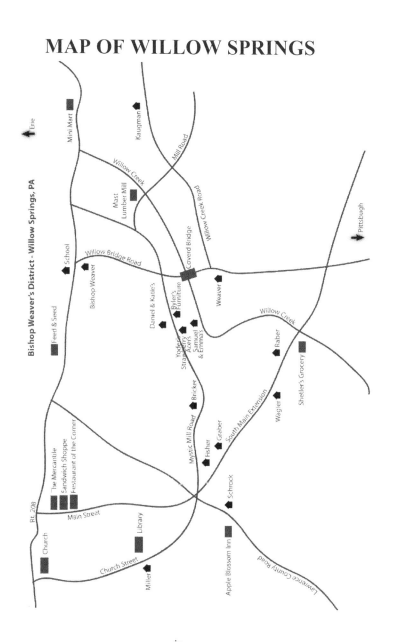

Bishop Weaver's District - Willow Springs, PA

Erie

Mini Mart

Kaugman

Willow Creek

Mill Road

Mast Lumber Mill

Willow Creek Road

Covered Bridge

Pittsbugh

School

Willow Bridge Road

Bishop Weaver

Daniel & Katie's

Byler's Furniture

Weaver

Feed & Seed

Yoder's Strawberry Acres

Samuel & Emma's

Willow Creek

Raber

Shetler's Grocery

Bricker

Wegier

Mystic Mill Road

South Main Extension

The Mercantile

Sandwich Shoppe

Restaurant of the Corner

Fisher

Graber

Rt. 208

Main Street

Library

Schrock

Church

Apple Blossom Inn

Church Street

Lawrence County Road

Miller

PROLOGUE

October - Willow Springs, Pennsylvania

Emma Yoder snuggled in close to her husband, Samuel, and rested her hand on his arm. She took in the slow rise of his chest and thanked God for all the blessings He provided during their first year of marriage. Trying not to wake him, she listened as the winter wind whistled around the small *doddi haus* they called home. Samuel and her *bruder*, Daniel, were spending long hours building their new house in the field next to Samuel's parents. No heat and short days were making progress slow.

In the wee hours right before dawn, Emma treasured the few moments of her husband's warmth before the alarm jolted him from slumber. As she lifted her knee and laid it across his thigh, a small jolt from her protruding tummy woke him.

In a raspy voice next to her ear Samuel said, "I swear that boy will come out running."

She moved her cheek to his chest, "What makes you so sure it's a boy?"

He moved a wisp of her honey blonde hair from his chin and kissed the top of her head. "Wishful thinking, I guess."

Emma knew his heart was set on a baby boy, and she hoped and prayed if it was a girl, he'd love her the same.

Samuel turned on his side until their noses touched. He kissed the center of her forehead and squeezed her tight. "You've made me the happiest man." Reaching between them, he patted her stomach. "This child is one of many that will fill our new home."

She lifted her head and kissed his chin. "I hope you still say that when the restless nights and diapers pile up."

A nervous giggle emerged from him. "Deprived of sleep, no problem. Diapers? I might need to go to the barn if I'm called to change too many of those."

Emma lifted her hand and pushed his chest, making him fall to his back. "Oh no, we're in this together! Cries, diapers, teething, colic, and bad behavior ...the whole gamut. If I don't get to pick and choose, neither do you!"

She rolled off the bed and grabbed her robe to cover her white cotton nightdress, as he engulfed her in a hug from behind. He nuzzled her neck with warm kisses and muttered. "I think I'd like to stay right here for the day."

"Oh no, you don't; you have a house to work on and chores to do."

She stood to flip her robe around her shoulders as Samuel rolled from the bed. He slapped her bottom and said, "I'll start the coffee."

Emma reached for the hairbrush, sat down on the bed, and undid the long braid that fell over her shoulder. With each stroke through her waist-length hair, she said a prayer of gratefulness. Her life, as she saw it, was perfect. Samuel was the man of her dreams; a new house, her best friend and sister-in-law Katie Miller living across the street, and she was seven months pregnant with their first child. In her eyes, God had truly blessed her. With her hair still down, she pulled her robe closed and headed to the kitchen. The white porcelain pot on the stove had already started to gurgle as Samuel set two cups on the counter.

She filled a tiny pitcher with cream and sat it near his place at the head of the table, and asked, "What are your plans today?"

"Daniel and I are going to work on the kitchen. He's been a big help, and if we keep at it, we'll be able to move in by the time the baby comes. But first, we have to pick up the kitchen cupboards from your *datt's* shop. If all goes well, we'll get those hung today."

Emma pulled both hands up to her chin and clapped as a smile encased her face.

Samuel responded to her enthusiasm, "I guess by that little happy dance, you're excited."

"Now, understand, I love living here, but to have my own kitchen and one you built for me, for sure and certain is a woman's dream."

"I'll hang cupboards every day if it keeps that smile on your face."

She poured the hot brown liquid into his cup and set the kettle on a trivet in the middle of the table. He pulled her into his lap. "I still think I should stay home today."

"No, not that again!" She pushed herself back up.

"I have work to do, and so do you. Katie's coming over; we're working on a new baby quilt, and I want to make some gingersnaps before she gets here. Let me make you breakfast so you can get out of here, and I can get to work."

"So, Katie comes, and I'm out the door. I see how I rank!"

She slapped him with the towel. "Don't be silly. No one is more important than you."

***

Samuel whistled as he pulled on his boots and pushed his bangs back before covering them with his black felt hat. He winked at Emma and closed the door behind him. An early winter storm left the steps and sidewalk with six inches of fresh snow, covering up a thin layer of ice. He skimmed the porch for the snow shovel and bucket of salt but remembered he'd left it on the back stoop. He didn't take the time to shovel it and caught himself slipping on the icy steps before heading to the barn.

Samuel tipped his head to block the wind as he ducked inside the metal building. His new family buggy sat just inside the door amongst the implements used for strawberry season. Wishing he could take the enclosed carriage instead of the open wagon, he effortlessly lifted a shaft in each hand and backed the cart out the double doors. Before he had a chance to walk to the horse barn, Emma called his name from the front porch.

She held up a thermos. "Samuel, your coffee."

Before he had a chance to holler back, *the steps were slippery*, he saw a flash of white as her nightclothes, and wheat-colored hair spilled to the ground.

"Emma... nooooo!"

As if in slow motion, he ran to the crumpled form lying at the bottom of the steps. He knelt, placed his hand under the back of Emma's head, and felt warmth penetrating his glove. His bellowing scream pierced the frozen air. "Heeeelp!"

CHAPTER 1

*M*amm always said we have no control over the words that fill the pages of our book, and only God holds the pen. If I could re-write my story, I would erase the past thirty days for certain.

No matter how hard I try, the only comfort I find these days is when I sit at the foot of these two wooden crosses. Samuel doesn't seem to understand my need to spend time here, and he's afraid I'm not surrendering to God's will. There must be more to following the Lord than succumbing to His will.

Quite frankly, I'm sick of hearing about God's will. I've had more than one well-meaning neighbor tell me how and what I should be feeling. While I'm grateful for the outpouring of support they've shown, how can most know anything about losing a child? For seven months, I carried James inside of me as he grew in anticipation of life, but in a split-second, he was gone.

Even now, as the cold penetrates my wool stockings' I yearn to hold him. My only comfort comes from laying him to rest on top of *Mamm's* grave. When I close my eyes, I imagine her snuggling him and keeping him warm when I can't. When reality hits, I'm reminded his cold, lifeless body was left to decay in the earth, much like my hopes and dreams for his future.

Not even the sun that warmed the earth the day we put James to rest could melt the ice lodged around my heart. I still remember the look of pity etched on the faces of my family and friends on that October morning.

Samuel held me up, as I shook, and we watched the pint-size pine coffin being placed in the ground. I couldn't move and prayed I'd wake up from the horrible nightmare as Samuel whispered in my ear. "God willing, this will be the hardest day we'll ever have to face."

Placing a child in a pine box changes you. I don't know how it couldn't. Even the dirt hitting the wood reminded me of all the things we wouldn't experience.

Thud.

No first smiles.

Thud.

No first steps.

Thud.

No first words.

Thud.

In the days that followed, my family and friends surrounded me, and I felt their love. In reality, I knew I wasn't left alone to bear the weight of our loss, but I pushed them all away. Especially Katie. Now the mere sight of her protruding belly makes me cringe. Doesn't she realize what we once had will never be again? Just being around her is exhausting. It takes every ounce I have to pretend I enjoy her company. I wish she would stop coming by. I suppose with her being family and all, that won't happen.

Maybe Samuel is right. I need to stop coming here. Is it helping? Probably not since I haven't seen another person in this cemetery in the four weeks I've been making my daily visits. Am I the only one who can't let go? Or maybe I'm the only Amish woman in these parts going against all we've been taught, like hiding our pain under layers and layers of fake smiles and forced hellos. If one more person tells me God makes no mistakes, I'll scream. Because in this case, He did, and I'm not sure I'll ever get over it.

Look at me, sitting here alone on the cold ground talking to myself; Samuel thinks I'm losing my mind, and I have to agree. Nothing he says comforts me, and I can feel him pulling away. How do couples survive this? Nobody should bury their child; it's just not right. I don't care what they say, I'm not yielding to God's will, I won't do it!

***

Walking the twenty minutes down Mystic Mill Road and back toward home, I pulled my heavy brown bonnet tighter around my chin. Snow from the dark clouds overhead started to cover the ground that reminded me of that fretful day just thirty days earlier. Alone with my grief, I screamed to the sky.

"What did you gain by taking him from me? You could have let him live. Why?"

Pittsburgh Memorial Hospital, 30 Days Earlier - October 15th

Caught somewhere between sleep and a dream, Emma tried to open her eyes to no avail. Voices in the room told her she wasn't alone, but she struggled to shake free from the hold unconsciousness had on her. An unfamiliar scent filled her nose, and the pounding in her head left her frozen in the strange surroundings. A constant beep replaced the murmur, and a gentle squeeze to her fingertips preceded a raspy whisper near her ear.

"Emma, please come back to me. Please, my love, wake up."

The urgency in Samuel's voice alarmed her, and she pushed through the last layer of darkness. Moving her thumb over the side of his finger, she turned her head toward his voice.

"Thank God, you're back."

Without opening her eyes, she asked, "Where am I?"

"At the hospital. Don't move; you have a nasty cut on the back of your head, and you have a concussion."

There was a heaviness in the room that told her all she needed to know long before she moved her hand to her sunken middle. She gave up the fight to open her eyes and drifted back to a place where only dreams would come true.

***

Samuel stood at the window in Emma's room overlooking the busy Pittsburgh highway. With each passing car, life went on, oblivious to his pain and the guilt he felt. The scene from four hours earlier played in his head. The pool of blood left in the snow from the gash on Emma's head wasn't half as bad as the puddle that seeped from her night dress when he picked her up. He was certain traces were still visible long after the ambulance had been summoned. With limited access to telephone and transportation, it took over an hour to get her help. The fall down the icy steps caused a placental abruption, and their baby died in the womb from a lack of oxygen. Even an emergency c-section didn't help in saving their first child's life. Because of his neglect, his son was gone, and he'd put his wife in danger. Collapsing in the brown leather chair, he buried his head in his hands and cried out.

"Please, Lord, help me make sense of all of this. If this is your will. Give me the wisdom to accept it gracefully no matter

how hard it is, and please help Emma wake up in time to say goodbye to our son. Amen"

When he lifted his face from his hands, Emma's eyes fluttered open. She turned her hand over and wiggled her fingers for him to come closer. He scurried to her bedside, fell to his knees, and laid his head on her chest. Her warmth comforted him for just a minute before the door opened and a nurse entered carrying a small blue bundle.

"I have him ready and can give you about an hour."

Samuel stood and held out his arms as the older woman laid the lifeless body in the crook of his elbow.

"Your family just arrived. I told them to give you both a few minutes alone with him. Do you want me to hold them off longer?"

"No, Emma will want to see them."

The nurse hesitated and then whispered, "I know how hard it is, but you both need to say your goodbyes quickly."

Without responding, he turned to face his wife.

They had made so many plans about how they would welcome their first child into the world, but none of them included this. Now standing at her bedside, all he could do was offer her a glimpse of what could have been.

She turned her head and moved her arm, so he could tuck the tiny-wrapped figure under her chin.

In a rattled whisper, she cried, "Oh, my baby, I'm sorry I failed you."

A sob lodged in the back of Samuel's throat as his wife took his blame. No words would come as Emma ran her finger over the child's transparent skin and examined his tiny fingers. When he didn't think he could manage another moment, she kissed his forehead and cried. "See you soon, sweet boy."

Her hollow brown eyes told him he was free to take him from her arms. When he scooped him up, she closed her eyes and turned further into her pillow and wept.

As long as he lived, he'd never forget the look in her eyes. Seeing her suffer so desperately with no relief in sight was dreadful. All he could do was dig deep into his faith and remember what he'd been taught ...many things in life were not meant to be understood. It wasn't his job to question God's plan but to humbly submit to His timing, no matter the circumstances.

**

It had been well over a month since she held her son in her arms, and even though she never felt his warm skin against her own, she ached to hold him. The wind whistled as it ran through the leafless trees, wrapping itself with a vengeance around her shoulders. Her heart ran cold, much like Willow Creek and its icy banks. Taking shelter under the timbers of the old, covered bridge, she let her voice bounce off the trusses in an agonizing cry. "Lord, why did you take James from me? Tell me why."

When nothing but silence filled the air, she followed the sound of Samuel and Daniel's hammers home. It wouldn't be long before they could move from the small *doddi haus* into the spacious farmhouse Samuel had worked hard to complete. The excitement had long-lost its appeal, and it was all she could do to pull herself out of bed, let alone think about moving into their new home without a child to fill it.

Emma sighed when she saw Ruth, her mother-in-law, walking to the mailbox. If she could only find a way to melt into the landscape and go home unnoticed. Ruth meant well, and her concern was genuine, but she was the last person Emma wanted to deal with on days like today.

Ruth waved. "How are you?"

Emma smiled but didn't answer.

Ruth placed her hand on Emma's arm. "There comes a time when living in the past is worse than living in the present."

Emma didn't need to ask Ruth to explain; she knew exactly what she was referring to. Samuel had made it very clear he wasn't happy about her daily visits to the cemetery, and she was sure he shared his concern with his parents.

Ruth wrapped her arm around Emma's shoulders and guided her down the driveway. "Come inside. I have something I want to give you."

Emma's feet moved, and she tried not to let the heaviness in her shoulders melt Ruth's gentle touch. It was one thing to wallow in self-pity, but to let her darkened mood spill over to Ruth was another thing altogether. She followed Ruth up the steps and closed the door behind them. Warmth encircled her as she took off her wool coat and pushed the wrinkles out of her black cape dress. Slipping out of her boots, she placed them neatly on the mat beside the door before following Ruth to the kitchen.

Ruth pointed to the stove. "Put on the kettle for tea while I run upstairs. I'll be right back."

Emma carried the white porcelain pot to the sink and blew out a long breath. The last thing she wanted was to make small talk with Samuel's mother. Waiting for the water to fill, she glanced out the window to see Katie making her way around the house to the back door. Emma's stomach lurched when Katie's waddle reminded her that Katie would be celebrating her own new arrival soon.

Snow swirled in under Katie's feet as she struggled to close the door with the basket she was carrying.

Emma rushed to her side. "Let me help."

"Thank you. I didn't realize this was so heavy when I decided to cart it all the way here. But then everything feels heavier these days."

Emma forced a smile and turned her back toward the sink. "Your *mamm* and I were just about to have tea. Would you like some?"

Katie plopped down in the closest chair and continued taking off her bonnet and mittens. "I stopped over at your house this morning. I was hoping we could spend the day together sorting through some recipes."

Emma took three cups from the cupboard and the wooden box filled with tea and placed them on the table. "I went for a walk."

Katie blew into her cupped hands and looked at Emma. "I would have gone with you."

How could she explain to Katie that the very sight of her expanding middle sent her down a spiraling tunnel of despair? Before she had a chance to come up with a response, Ruth made her way back to the kitchen carrying a large white box.

"Katie, what a nice surprise. I didn't hear you come in."

Katie turned toward her mother's voice. "I brought over all my recipe books. I was hoping we could go through them to find some new recipes to try before the bakery opens back up." Katie ran small circles across her belly with the palm of her hand. "I'm a bit restless, and I'm trying to keep busy while we wait on this little one to arrive."

Without realizing it, Emma let out a small moan and covered her mouth with her hand as soon as it escaped her lips.

Katie reached her hand across the table and squeezed Emma's forearm. "I'm so sorry."

Emma pulled away. "You have nothing to be sorry about."

Ruth pulled the cover off the box in front of her. "I think trying a few new recipes is just what the doctor ordered for a day like today. But first, I have something I need to give to Emma."

She pushed the box across the table and pulled a chair up beside her. "I've been trying to find the right time to give this to you. The summer you were in Sugarcreek visiting your biological family, your mother crocheted three shawls. One for you, and one for both Rebecca and Anna. She knew there would come a time when each of you would need to feel her close. She knew then that her time on earth was short. I promised to give it to each of you when I felt you needed a piece of her the most."

Emma pulled the tightly weaved yarn from the box and held it to her cheek. The softness against her skin reminded her of her mothers' touch. Closing her eyes, she moved it to her nose, hoping a little piece of her lingered between the fibers. Deeply etched in the stitches, the faint sweetness of cherry and almonds tickled her nose. For sure and certain, it was the familiar scent of her *mamm's* hand lotion. Ruth slid a pink envelope across the table and motioned for Katie to follow her to the other room.

Tears clouded Emma's eyes as she recognized her *mamm's* delicate penmanship. Laying the cream-colored shawl across her lap, she reached for the letter.

Emma,

While I am not there to help you in this most challenging time, you need to know there is someone you can lean on. Someone who I did not get to know until just a short time ago. My heart aches that I will not be there to share the truth with you. Please know you are good enough, and you will see life without pain and turmoil in heaven, regardless of how obedient you were on earth. But first, you must let Jesus into your heart and rely on Him for your salvation.

This may confuse you for a short time. But regardless of the turmoil it may cause, search for the truth in Jesus.

My prayer is that you will wrap yourself in this shawl and remember my words as you search for a relationship with Jesus. He is there to help you every step of the way ...all you have to do is ask.

All my love,

Mamm

Emma placed the letter back in its holder, tucked it deep inside the box, folded the shawl, and secured it beneath the layers of tissue paper. She slipped her feet in her boots and tied her coat and bonnet before heading out the door. Without looking back, Emma held her *mamm's* gift in her gloved hands and walked home. A single tear rolled down her cheek as she whispered, *"I'm not sure how Jesus can help me through any of this. It's my fault. I must have done something to upset God for Him to take James from me. I don't understand and I have no energy to search for the truth you speak of. I just wish you were here to explain it all to me. Oh,* Mamm, *I miss you so!"*

CHAPTER 2

K atie stood at the window and sipped her tea as Emma walked down the driveway.

"I don't know what to do. I keep trying to reach out, but she keeps pushing me away. Even Daniel has tried, but we can't seem to make any headway with her."

Ruth moved a stack of fabric from the chair near the window so her daughter could sit. "You have to realize she may be having a hard time connecting with you right now. You shared the one thing that was taken from her. In her eyes, you are a constant reminder of all she lost. Give her some time; she'll come around."

Katie sat up straight and rubbed her lower back. "I miss her."

Ruth picked up a pair of scissors and cut around the paper pattern pinned to the black broadcloth fabric that would soon be a new pair of pants for her husband, Levi.

"It's hard to watch someone you care about go through something like this. All you can do is be there for her. I learned a long time ago that the one thing a person needs when something so traumatic happens is just time. Time to grieve. Time to heal. And time to accept the outcome."

"But it's been over a month, and I don't see her coming to terms with any of it."

Ruth sat in the chair behind the black treadle sewing machine. "You have to realize that losing a child is like losing a part of yourself. Your arms ache to hold the one thing that grew under your heart for so long. We might not always understand God's ways, but we must believe He has a plan, even when we can't see a way out of our grief. That's what Emma is going through right now. She can't figure out a way to escape her heartache, and she blames herself."

Katie shifted in the chair and rested her hand across her belly. "I thought talk of opening the bakery back up would help occupy her mind some. But I'm not even excited about that. I just don't know what to say. What do you say to a mother who came home childless?"

Ruth unpinned the brown paper from the fabric and slipped it under the sewing foot of the machine. Using her hands to guide the material, she pumped the treadle to put the needle in motion. "Not much you can say. All you can do is listen when she is ready to talk. Maybe the letter from Stella will help."

Katie stood back at the window that overlooked her parents' farm. From her mother's upstairs sewing room, she had views of both her and Daniel's house across the street, along with the tiny house next to the barn where Emma and Samuel were living.

"So much sadness in her eyes. I'm not sure any of us will get through to her. Even with Christmas being just a few weeks away, I find it hard to be excited for much of anything with Emma feeling so poorly."

Slowing the treadle machine down while she turned the fabric to sew the next seam, Ruth added, "Maybe I should write to Marie. A girl needs her mother at a time like this. With Stella being gone, maybe her biological mother can help pull her through this when we can't. Marie couldn't make it for the funeral with her husband's mother being so ill, but maybe she can come now."

"What a great idea. Emma loves Marie. A visit from her might be just what she needs. Maybe if she can't come here, Emma could go to Sugarcreek. A few days away from all the memories would help. It would give Daniel and Samuel a chance to put in some long hours on the house. They could have it done by the time she got back. That would cheer her up for sure."

Katie walked to her mother and placed a kiss on her cheek. "Thanks, *Mamm*, you always know the right thing to do."

"Now, don't get ahead of yourself. I'm not sure if Marie can come, or if she'd be up for a visit from Emma with her being so busy taking care of her mother-in-law. But I'll send a letter right off to her this afternoon."

Katie walked to the door and said, "I best go home to Daniel. He'll be coming in for lunch soon, and I want to tell him of your plans. I'll be praying all the way home it works out, and we see a smile on Emma's face again real soon."

***

Emma carried the box to the top of the stairs and stood in the hallway between the bedroom she shared with Samuel and the closed door of the child she never welcomed home. Pushing the slightly ajar door to her room open with her hip, she dropped the box on the bed and flipped the cover off. Her mother's note fell to the floor. Picking up the handmade item and draping it around her shoulders, she curled up in a ball at the foot of her bed. She couldn't even find the strength to cry again in the nightmare that wouldn't stop. Burying her head deeper in the crook of her arm, she murmured, *"I'm so confused. What are you trying to teach me, Mamm? Losing James is too much to bear. I'm too tired to figure your message out. My heart hurts so bad ...the pain is unbearable. I just want to be with you...and James."*

Sleep once again dulled the pain.

***

Like being dragged from the murky waters of a deep pond, Emma pulled herself to a sitting position when she heard Samuel's voice.

"Emma? Where are you?"

Without answering, she neatly folded the shawl and placed it back inside the box. Scooting it under the bed, she picked up the pink envelope and tucked it in her apron pocket before heading to the door. Willing herself to face the tension that had built up between her and Samuel, she filled her lungs with a deep breath and followed his call.

Avoiding his eyes, she brushed by him and moved to the stove. "I didn't give much thought to dinner. I hope tomato soup and toasted cheese is okay?"

The chair's wooden legs scraped across the polished pine floor as he pulled it away from the table and patted the chair next to him. "Come sit. We need to talk."

A heaviness in the air magnified his words to a point she had no choice but comply.

"Bishop Weaver paid me a visit today."

"And?"

"He asked about you and how you were feeling."

"That was nice of him, but I'm sure he had more to say."

"He did. He saw you revisiting the cemetery and is concerned I'm not leading my family in the ways of the *Ordnung*. He made it clear that the rules of our ways are to be followed, in both good and bad times."

She twisted the towel in her hands and waited for him to finish.

"He firmly but politely informed me that I must stop you from visiting James' graveside. He is afraid the community will take it as if you are not trusting in God's plan. Which will not be healthy for the members of the church."

In a soft whisper, she asked, "How is it anyone's business how I spend my days?"

"It is not our way, and the bishop won't tolerate your outward display. Just as we are to forgive our neighbors, he expects you to forgive God and accept whatever He places in front of us with grace and humility. Emma, He knows best, I'm sure of it."

Emma stood, pushed her chair in with more force than necessary, and walked to the sink, holding herself up by cupping the edge of the basin. "I refuse to push James so far from my mind I forget what his face looked like. How dare he think my pain is so shallow that I can move past it in a few short weeks?"

Samuel walked up behind her and wrapped his arms around her middle. "Your pain is real; I feel it too. But we must trust God makes no mistakes."

Rotating from his embrace, she snarled. "Not you too! How can you accept our son's death so easily? He was a living person for seven months; right here under my heart. We felt him kick, we talked to him, we made plans for his future. And in a moment, God took him from us, without even giving us a chance to hold his warm body. How can that be from God? And if it was, we must have done something to anger Him!"

Samuel tried to pull her in close, but she pushed him away and ran to the steps, only stopping to look his way for a moment. "You both can stifle my sorrow from the community, but you can't shield my heart from the pain I feel in these empty arms and full bosom. I'll never accept it. I won't. I promise you that!"

Her bare feet slapped against the cold wooden steps and didn't stop until the bedroom door rattled against its hinges.

Samuel laid his head on his folded arms on the edge of the table. How was he ever going to help Emma through this? Guilt magnified every time he saw the pain in her eyes. Maybe she was right. Perhaps, they had done something to upset God. Why else would he take their son from them?

His mind raced ...

If only he had worked harder.

If only he had followed the rules better.

If only he would have salted the steps.

If only he had remembered to pick up his thermos.

If only he would have ...what? Anything but be the one responsible?

The fear of not knowing what to do was exhausting, but the sound of Emma crying herself to sleep each night was heart-wrenching. It was almost more than he could handle. He knew he should go upstairs and comfort her, but instead, he grabbed his hat off the hook by the back door and went to work.

***

By the time Emma woke from her sleep-induced coma, the day had turned into night. A chill in the house reminded her she needed to add coal to the furnace, and a growl in her tummy prompted her to start supper. Brushing the sleep from her eyes, she focused on the windup clock on the nightstand. Ten o'clock? Turning toward Samuel's side of the bed, she felt his spot. The cold sheets told her he must have retreated to the daybed set up in the front room. After her earlier outburst, she couldn't blame him. But sleeping all afternoon and through supper was unacceptable, even if she had lost her desire to be a good wife.

There was an icy edge to the air, and she wondered why Samuel hadn't stoked the fire. Pulling the extra blanket from the foot of the bed and wrapping it around her shoulders, she headed downstairs. Not even the moon against the snow-covered ground filtered light into the pitch-black kitchen. She fumbled, lighting the lantern above the table, and knocked a jar of peanut butter across the table. By the looks of it, Samuel had fixed himself a sandwich before turning in. A sudden urge to find comfort in her husband's arms forced her to walk to the front room. His blanket and pillow were still neatly folded in the same spot they had been earlier. It was after ten, where could he be? She certainly couldn't blame him if he didn't want to come home. Half the time, she didn't want to be there herself.

***

Daniel had long left, and Samuel struggled to fasten the last cabinet to the wall by himself. After installing the furnace ducts two days ago, he could light a fire in the coal stove in the basement. If he couldn't help Emma, he could at least work hard to finish their new home before Christmas. He hoped the new house would avert her attention away from James and back to the present. There was no doubt in his mind he was working in survival mode, but it was the only thing he knew he could control.

His earlier conversation with Bishop Weaver left him feeling inadequate as a husband and leader of his family. Thoughts of how he failed Emma consumed every waking minute. Throwing himself into the house was all he knew how to do.

The back door swung open, and a burst of snow swirled around his father's feet.

"Boy, what are you doing still working? You should be home with Emma."

"I could turn it around. You should be home with *Mamm*."

"I saw the light on over here and wanted to check on you. Whatever you're working on can wait until tomorrow."

"I wanted to finish hanging this last cupboard, then I was going to call it a day."

Levi picked up the drill and tightened the last two screws while Samuel held it in place. He leaned into the battery-operated drill and asked, "Jacob did a great job. Has Emma seen them yet?"

"She has no interest in seeing what her father crafted for us."

"Your *Mamm* made her come in for tea this morning, but she left as soon as she opened Stella's gift."

Samuel checked the level one more time before stepping back. "A gift from her mother? She didn't mention it. But I suppose I didn't give her a chance before I told her about my visit with the bishop."

Levi picked up some tools off the floor and laid them on the counter. "I saw his buggy here this morning. I assumed he was checking on your progress."

"He did walk through the house, but he was more concerned about my control over my household."

Levi leaned back on the counter and crossed his arms over his chest. "What?"

"It doesn't look good to the community if Emma is still holding on to the past. He's afraid she hasn't succumbed to God's will. He was sympathetic to her pain but advised me to forbid her from making any more trips to the cemetery."

Levi furrowed his eyebrows. "That's why they encourage daily visits from the community. If she's struggling, she needs to accept the help from those checking in on her. No one should be alone in times like this. Has she let any of the women visit?"

"No, and they stopped coming. Emma let them in the first few days, but she refused to answer the door after that. She's even shut Katie out."

Samuel sat on the rung of the ladder. "I don't know what to do."

Levi stepped closer and placed a hand on Samuel's shoulder. "Son, none of us were born knowing exactly what it takes to be the head of a family. Some days are easier than others, but the key is to get out of God's way the best we can."

"Get out of God's way?"

"You know, like when your horse leads you one way when you want to go another? Most times he saw something in the road you didn't. It's the same with God. Many things in this life aren't meant to be understood. We simply aren't strong enough to bear knowing it all. Where there are gaps in our understanding, there is grace in knowing He carries all our burdens, no matter how big or small."

"How can I convince Emma to see that?"

Levi tugged on his beard. "I'm not sure. But in those times when I thought there was no way out, He showed me something greater than I could ever have imagined."

Samuel rested his elbows on his knees and clasped his hands together. "She has closed herself off from me and our marriage."

"I don't have an answer, but He will. Take it to the Lord and then wait. It takes great patience and faith to go through each day expecting to hear from Him."

"I've been doing that over and over again; nothing but crickets. When something does come to mind, I can't be sure if it's God reaching out or my own thoughts."

Levi propped his foot upon a turned-over bucket and leaned on his knee. "Not too long-ago Bishop Weaver preached on hearing from God. Do you remember that?"

"*Jah*, but I couldn't tell you specifically what he said."

"If we are unsure of what we are hearing is from God, we need to ask ourselves these few things. One, does what you hear line up with Scripture? Two, does it line up with messages you hear from church? And lastly, would it please God?"

Samuel stood and took off his tool belt and put on his jacket. "I'd forgotten about those three questions."

Levi headed to the door. "Look, I believe the Lord orchestrates all things for good. And even though losing James seems too big for Emma right now, I guarantee you at some point, you'll look back and realize the good that came from his death."

Samuel reached for the doorknob but hesitated. "*Datt* do you believe God punishes us?"

Levi studied Samuel. "Why do you ask?"

"No reason, just wondering."

Levi rested his hand on his shoulder. "Lord willing, we will do all He asks of us, and we'll stand before Him one day, and it won't matter."

Samuel stood in the doorway and waved goodnight to his father. Before turning down the kerosene light, he uncovered the book on the counter he and Daniel had been reading together and tucked it in a drawer out of sight. He pondered Emma's statement about them angering God on the short walk back home. He promised to protect her and his family, and he failed both so far. His stomach lurched as he kicked the snow off his boots before stepping in out of the cold.

CHAPTER 3

Emma hadn't left home in the two weeks since Bishop Weaver's visit. No visits with Katie, no walks, not even a trip to town. Samuel had all but given up on pulling her outside. The last few days, he made a point to be long gone before she wandered downstairs and didn't come home until she had gone to bed. It was all she could do to fix an evening meal and leave it on the stove. She was sure his mother was feeding him the forenoon meal since he gave up coming in for dinner.

Hammers and saws echoed in the air long into the night. Resentment filled those dark hours as she found herself lying alone. Samuel's lack of emotion was frustrating, and she couldn't fathom how he could be so callous about all they had lost. Her heart was breaking while he hammered away, building a future she couldn't imagine. She was certain he was burying his grief the only way he knew how. But all she could count on was that he wasn't lying beside her, holding her close or reassuring her they'd get through it. How was it he could deal with it so much better than she? Or maybe he was just better at hiding it. Whatever the case, she built a wall around herself, even true love couldn't break through.

***

Sun filtered through the blue-pleated curtain, forcing Emma to open her eyes. Illuminated dust danced in the beam of light, and for a moment, the heaviness in her chest disappeared.

The smell of coffee and bacon woke her stomach with a loud growl. She closed her eyes and tried to remember what day it was. Friday? No, Saturday? The clang of pans startled her to a sitting position while she rubbed the sleep from her eyes. Samuel's voice bounced up to her from below. "OUCH!"

Grabbing her robe from the end of the bed, she slipped it over her shoulders as she ran downstairs. Smoke forced her to open the window above the sink. "Are you trying to burn the house down?"

"I was mixing up the eggs, and the bacon burned. I only had my back to it for a minute."

Emma twisted her hair in a long coil and tucked it in the back of her housecoat before grabbing the towel from Samuel's hand. "Sit, let me finish this before you make a bigger mess."

She wrapped the towel around the handle of the cast-iron pan and slid it to the back of the stove. Using the towel as a fan, she waved the smoke out the open window before heading to the back door to do the same.

Samuel had another towel flipped over his shoulder and egg on his shirt. "I wanted to surprise you, but then I burned my hand, and ...well, you know the rest."

For a split-second, it was like the last six weeks ceased to exist. His boyish grin and dimpled chin charmed her into a smile.

"You're helpless when it comes to women's work. Why would you even try?"

"I was hoping I'd see a smile."

"Well, you saw it, now off with you."

She walked to the bowl on the counter and ran a fork through it. "These eggs are filled with shells. Please, go to your mother's and get some more."

Samuel stood and rolled his hand off the top of his head and bowed. "Your wish is my command, princess."

She slapped him with the towel. "Quit ...just go so I can clean up this mess."

Without a jacket, he stepped in his boots and ran across the yard to his parents' house.

Emma watched his long strides in the deep snow and giggled when he tripped. The sun was glistening off the frozen ground, making its way to meet the bluebird sky that made a beautiful backdrop to the frosted trees.

The coffee started to gurgle against the glass globe, and she turned down the heat and glanced at the clock. Samuel liked his coffee strong, but anything past five minutes would make it bitter. She couldn't remember the last time she'd fixed breakfast, but it felt good to tend to her husband's needs. No sooner had she wiped the table and put fresh bacon in a clean pan, Samuel came bounding in the back door. Cold had added color to his cheeks, and his boots left traces of snow on the floor before he kicked them off in the corner.

He placed the bowl of eggs on the counter and pulled her close. Without saying a word, he held her tight, and she relaxed in his arms as he kissed the top of her head. Tears welled in the corner of her eyes, and she swallowed hard to push all that came between them away. There was so much to explain, but she wasn't ready to give up on their dreams just yet. Stepping back from his embrace, she picked up the eggs and carried them to the stove.

Lifting the porcelain coffee pot, she poured him a cup and set it in front of him. Before she had a chance to walk away, he grabbed her hand. The longing in his eyes was filled with desire. But she moved her head from side to side and pulled her hand from his. Turning her attention back to the bacon, she felt the air in the room turn cold, much like his tone the minute he spoke.

"Bishop Weaver expects us back in church tomorrow. He says six weeks is long enough."

She cracked four eggs in a bowl and whipped them with a fork with her back toward him. She chewed her bottom lip as he continued.

"Church is at the Schrocks'. The paper said the temperature won't be out of the twenties today, so if Eli's hill is still ice-covered, we'll need to go the way of Willow Bridge. Might take us up to an hour, so we'll leave by seven-thirty."

Emma closed her eyes and braced herself for his rebuttal. "I'm not going."

"What?"

Without turning to face him she said, "I'm not going. The last thing I want is a bunch of old women whispering about me behind my back or telling me how I should be feeling."

Samuel stood, pushed his chair in, slammed it against the table, and walked beside her. He cupped her face in his calloused hands. "Emma, James was God's child to give and His to take back. He loved him more than we can ever comprehend."

Emma reached up and tried to pull his hands from her cheeks, but he held tighter and pulled her forehead into his. "We must trust in His plan, and you will go to church tomorrow."

Emma twisted from his grasp and dropped to a chair as he bent to whisper in her ear. "Life goes on, and the sooner you realize that the better. I strongly suggest you get out of this house today. Go to Katie's or visit your *datt*."

She turned her head away from his breath and murmured. "How come you're not angry?"

He slipped his feet back in his boots and pushed his arms through his black wool coat. "Who says I'm not angry? I'm upset at what it's doing to you and to us."

Samuel held his hand on the doorknob and paused. "Anger won't bring him back." A burst of cold air fluttered across her bare feet as he pulled the door shut behind him.

Life was sucked out of the room, and she stood to move the frying pans off the fire. She poured herself a cup of coffee and carried it to the front room.

The purple and white quilt from the back of the rocking chair fell to the floor when she pulled the chair closer to the window with her foot. Setting the cup on the stand, she wrapped the hand-stitched blanket around her shoulders and picked back up the mug. The steam from the dark liquid bounced off her nose when she blew over the rim. Tears spilled over her eyelashes, and she blinked to let them fall. They rolled down her cheeks and landed on the point of the broken star pattern on the quilt. The jagged points of the star matched her brokenness.

Setting the cup back down, she wiped the moisture away from *Mommi* Lillian's tiny stitches on the quilt she'd made for her. She yearned for her grandmother's face. There was a calmness that came over her every time she received a letter.

Lillian had a way of seeing past all the bad in the world. Even after *Doddi* Melvin passed, she found things to bring her joy. Oh, how she wished she could find the same peace her grandmother spoke of.

A cardinal outside the window caught her attention as she thought; *losing a husband can't be as bad as losing a child. Can it?* The red bird reminded her of the stained ice she stepped over when Samuel brought her home. He'd spent two hours scraping the spot away as she lay in bed, lost in a fog.

The bird flew away when Ruth walked up to the porch and waved at Emma through the window. Without knocking, she let herself in.

"I was just out to the phone shanty, and there was a message from Marie for you."

Emma grabbed a tissue from the box near her chair. "Did she say what she wanted?"

Ruth looked tenderly toward her daughter-in-law. "I'm sure your birth mother is worried about you like we all are."

Emma stared back out the window and whispered, "I can't give Samuel what he needs."

Ruth slipped out of her coat and headscarf before coming to sit in the chair next to Emma. "You're way too hard on yourself."

Ruth took Emma's hand and squeezed it ever so lightly. "I understand what you are going through. While I didn't lose a baby as far along as you did, I had my fair share of miscarriages between Samuel and Katie."

Emma turned and looked back out the window. "Motherhood won't happen for me ...the way ...I always dreamed it would."

"It will, I promise you that."

Emma choked on a sob and hiccupped between her words. "You can't ...promise me ...that.

"No, I suppose I can't. Emma, you need to reach out to Samuel, he is hurting too, and you need to face this together. You can't let this come between you both."

"But ...he didn't ...bond to James like I did."

"True, maybe he didn't. But he loves you, and if you are hurting, so is he."

Emma blew her nose and took in a deep breath. "I don't know how ...to weave past the ...pain."

Emma placed her hand over her chest. "How do I stop ...loving him?"

Ruth's eyes clouded over. "Oh my. You never have to stop loving him. He will always be a part of you, even though he is in his forever home now. Don't expect a day to go by when you don't think about him, especially this early on, nor should you want to. Don't put a time limit on your recovery, but you do have to continue to live."

"But ...you don't ...understand."

"I do. There will be more children. And you and Samuel will get through this, I promise you that."

Emma focused on the birds. "Thank you ...for delivering ...Marie's message."

Ruth laid her hand on Emma's shoulder. "I'm here for you if you need me, but perhaps a phone call to Marie would do you some good. A girl needs her mother in times like this. She's not Stella, but I'm certain she loves you just the same."

The door closed, and Ruth's long black coat swayed behind her as she made her way across the yard. An array of thoughts swirled around Emma's head. *She doesn't understand ...no one can. There will be no more children for me, James was the only son I will ever bear, and I have no one to blame but myself...and God.*

The words of Dr. Smithson haunted her every day since her two-week checkup. "Emma, you do understand you'll need to wait twenty-four months before getting pregnant again. You need to give your body enough time to heal. If you don't, you could risk the life of another child and have a series of complications that could hinder you from ever conceiving again."

What he was asking her to do was far beyond anything the bishop would approve. The use of birth control was not allowed, no matter the circumstances. In all things, she was taught to look to the Lord to provide and protect. That included bringing children into the world. How would she explain to Samuel she couldn't share their marriage bed for two years? The thought of losing another child far outweighed the disappointment in Samuel's face when he learned of Dr. Smithson's warning.

For days, Samuel had been begging her to come see the progress on their new house. How could she explain the empty rooms would always be void of laughter? His hopes and dreams of little housekeepers and farmhands would never come true. The burden of keeping the doctor's recommendations to herself only added to her state of mind.

Marie wasn't the mother who raised her, but she was, in all rights, her mother. Maybe a visit to her birth mother's home in Sugarcreek was just what she needed.

***

The gray skies of winter hailed a flood of emotions as Emma used straight pins to fasten her black mourning dress closed. Samuel was adamant they attend church service, and no amount of pleading on her part would soften his request. His refusal to listen to her reasoning only added to the distance they now shared.

The long braid she twisted and secured at the nape of her neck matched the knot in her stomach. No amount of covering could calm her nerves as she struggled to pin the starch white *kapp* in place. A quick tug on the curtain revealed Samuel had the family buggy waiting outside. Taking a moment to watch the scene unfold, she yearned for Samuel's touch.

There was a gentleness in the way Samuel ran his hand over Oliver, their buggy horse. The muscular animal leaned into Samuel as he checked his bit and ran a hand over the length of Oliver's mane. Oliver neighed and lifted his head toward Samuel's voice when he whispered something in his ear, which relaxed the horse's posture even more. There was no doubt Samuel and Oliver shared a deep relationship that was built on trust and understanding. A pang of envy coiled around her heart as Samuel readied the horse.

A deep breath filled her lungs, preparing herself to face Samuel. Their late-night argument left her uneasy about the hour-long ride to the Schrocks'. Furthermore, her refusal to answer the door when Maggie and others came calling left her apprehensive about seeing them. Many of her friends were swollen with motherhood which would be like adding salt to an open wound. She was finding it hard to breathe in anticipation of the pain it would cause.

The squeak of the front door preceded Samuel's voice.

"Emma, let's go. We'll be late if we don't leave right now."

He held her coat open, so she could slip her arms in and handed her the heavy brown bonnet to cover her prayer *kapp*.

"Denki," was all she could muster as she followed him down the front steps.

No amount of tension would interfere with Samuel's responsibility to her comfort. Once he helped her inside, he tucked a blanket over her lap and moved the warm bricks he had added to the floorboards closer to her feet to keep her warm.

Before picking up the reins, he reached over and squeezed her gloved hand. With a flick of the leather strap and a click of his tongue, Oliver followed Samuel's lead and moved the carriage forward. How could an animal as large as the dark brown standardbred so easily conform to Samuel's will? The only word that came to mind was *trust.*

Samuel tried his best to lighten the mood as they made their way over the ice-covered driveway. He waved in his father's buggy direction and tipped his hat at Daniel and Katie as they pulled out behind them. "Daniel's been a big help the last couple of weeks. Not sure how I would have gotten so much done on the house without him."

"Jah."

She felt him stiffen a bit before he asked, "Perhaps you might like to see the cabinets your *datt* made for us later today?"

"Nee."

He didn't say a word as he stared motionlessly ahead. His eyebrows curled against each other, and his eyes narrowed with disappointment. "I'll have the house completed in less than a week. You'll need to start packing up our things to move out of the *doddi haus* soon. Most likely before Christmas."

The remainder of their ride was in silence as Emma fought the urge to throw herself from the moving buggy. The last thing she wanted to do was move into their new house without James, let alone face the pitiful eyes of her community that morning.

Samuel pulled up to the young boy in charge of unhitching the horses and parking the buggies. Emma sat still as Samuel walked around the horse to unsnap the brown canvas covering the door and help her down. The line of women forming at Maggie's side door looped around the front porch of the white clapboard farmhouse. Men had gathered at the foot of the stairs waiting for the women to file in first. Without parting words, both she and Samuel headed in different directions.

Katie walked up beside her and wrapped her arm around her shoulders. "I'm glad to see you."

Her elbow brushed Katie's protruding stomach, and she pulled away from her embrace and whispered. "I didn't have much choice in the matter."

"Come now, it won't be that bad. Samuel is only doing what the bishop is instructing him to do. You can't fault him for following the rules of the *Ordnung*."

Emma stopped and grabbed Katie's hand. "How did you know about that?"

"Daniel told me. I suppose Samuel needed a friend to talk to, and he confided in your *bruder*."

Emma clicked her tongue and moved forward. Katie rushed to catch up to her and leaned in so only she could hear. "Isn't that what good friends do? They talk to one another."

Emma didn't respond but continued to make her way through the back door. She stepped around a group of women just inside the door. Making her way to the women's side of the room, Emma took a seat next to the wall. Keeping her hands folded over the *Ausbund* songbook during the first song, she waited until the Lob Lied's first words were sung before joining in. The German hymn was the second song sang at every Amish church service across the country. Typically, she loved its long drawn-out verses, but today she found no comfort when the words echoed off the barren walls; forcing a lump to settle in the back of her throat.

Katie sang the words ...*Gib unserm Herzen auch Verstand* and reached over and patted the top of her hand. The words, *give our hearts, also, understanding* meant nothing to her, and she pulled her hand away.

A whimper of a small child caught her attention, and she followed the sound to Maggie Schrock, who quietly rocked her two-month-old and patted his small back to calm his cry. Emma gently mimicked her motion, but her arms were empty. She closed her eyes and thought. *My body can't accept it any more than my heart can.*

CHAPTER 4

Samuel pulled the buggy to a stop and secured the reins before jumping down to help Emma. For hours, he studied her from across the room while she endured the message. It wasn't hard to recognize the words were meant solely for her. They matched almost precisely to the conversations he had tried to have with her on several occasions. Letting the words fill the dead space between them on the way home did little to comfort her. He regretted repeating the words, now that she was even more distant than she was earlier. He hoped to remind her that God's ways were not always ours, but we still needed to trust He knows best. It was no help and he found little hope in the words himself.

Unsnapping the heavy yellow canvas, then pulling it aside, he lent a hand while she stepped down from the enclosed buggy.

When she slipped and fell into him, she buried her head in his chest and kept it there for a few seconds before pushing herself back. He wrapped his hand around her waist and pulled her close.

"Why pull away? I'm your husband, and there is no shame in leaning on me."

She pushed her hand against his torso. "You invited Daniel and Katie to spend the afternoon with us. I need to make coffee."

"They went home first, so we have a few minutes. He kept one hand firmly pressed on her lower back and took his other hand to place a finger beneath her chin. "Look at me, Emma. I refuse to let our circumstances come between us."

Her beautiful brown eyes were dark, much like the sorrow etched in her expression. He bent down, rested his lips near hers, and breathed, "Please, my love, we need each other."

Without allowing him to kiss her or respond to his plea, she ducked under his arm and headed inside.

Samuel grabbed the harness close to Oliver's neck and guided him to the barn.

"Why can't she be more like you, my friend? You don't cringe at my touch." The horse pulled his head back and let out a soft whinny as if he understood Samuel's question.

After unhitching Oliver from the carriage, he led him to the stall and went to work brushing him down and filling his feed bucket. His smooth coat and gentle response soothed Samuel's lonely soul. He couldn't wrap his head around Emma's reaction to his touch. But more importantly ...how was he going to get them through this?

***

Emma was appalled that Samuel had invited Daniel and Katie to spend the afternoon with them. It was the last thing she wanted to deal with, and she'd rather spend the afternoon in bed. Rummaging through the cupboard for a box of store-bought cookies, she arranged them on a tray and placed four cups on the table.

Katie tapped on the window a few times before she opened the side door and let herself in. "Burr ...I swear the day is getting colder even if the thermometer says different." She shook off her coat, hung it on the peg near the door, and took a seat at the table before slipping out of her boots.

"Thank you so much for inviting us. It's been way too long since we've spent any time together. I miss you."

Emma placed a napkin under each mug around the table. "You can thank Samuel, not me."

Katie raised an eyebrow. "Would you rather I leave?"

"*Nee,* I just wanted to be sure you knew it was Samuel's idea, not mine."

Katie held her cup up while Emma filled it. "I'm not sure how you'll react to anything I say these days. I feel like I have to tread so lightly around you ...it never used to be like that."

Emma put the pot back on the stove and sat down beside her friend. "I'm so sorry. I just can't seem to break free from this dark cloud over me."

Katie reached behind her and rubbed her lower back and rested her hand on her stomach. "We haven't been best friends our whole life for me not to realize how much it bothers you seeing me like this. We've dreamed about this forever ...marriage and motherhood."

Emma propped her elbows up on the table and rested her chin over her clasped fingers. "Yet in our dreams, we never thought we'd have to face something like this."

"True, we didn't, but I can't help to think God is using this experience for a purpose. There just has to be a reason James left this world so soon."

"I can't grasp what that might be. How can taking a child from his mother without even letting her feel his warm body against her skin be for something good?"

"I don't have an answer, but you'll never know what He has planned or how He will use you until you let Him."

Emma dropped her head and rested her forehead on her folded hands and shook her head from side to side. "The pain is too raw to make any sense of it."

Emma sat back in the chair and wrapped her hands around the warm mug. "Everything upsets me. I'm mad when Samuel doesn't hold me, I pull back when he tries, but mostly, I'm heartbroken he seems so callous about it all. He acts like James meant nothing to him, like he didn't even exist."

Katie stirred a spoon of sugar in her coffee. "Now, just wait a minute. You have it all wrong. If you think for one minute he isn't hurting, you're sadly mistaken. I think he's trying to deal with his part in all of it. He blames himself for your fall down the steps in the first place."

"That was an accident and by no means his fault. I was the one who walked outside in my stocking feet. If anyone should be at blame, it should be me."

Emma paused to blow over the rim of her cup. "He's been working so hard on the house. Like he wants to forget James altogether."

"Again, my friend, you have it all wrong. If I haven't learned anything else in the past year being married to your *bruder*, I learned we don't process things the same way."

"What do you mean?"

"Men work through things by doing, not thinking. Women work through things by thinking, not doing. We shut ourselves out, stop doing, so we can work through our pain. Men don't stop to think, but they pick up a saw, or a hammer, or a fence post, and physically work through things with their body."

"I suppose that's why he's been so set on finishing our house, *jah?*"

"Exactly. As women, we hold on to things that could have been. Where a man is driven to "*do*" something to forget the pain."

Emma moved from the table and stared out the window above the sink. "There's more, but I'm not sure I should share it with you before talking to Samuel."

Emma let the room fill with silence while she contemplated whether to tell Katie what Dr. Smithson advised. Before she responded, Katie closed the gap. "If you have something you must share with my *bruder* first, please don't tell me. You need to go to God and then your husband."

Emma turned to face her. "I suppose you're right." She pulled out the drawer beside her and handed Katie the pink envelope that held her mother's letter. "Read this. It was tucked in the box your *mamm* gave me the other day."

Katie unfolded the paper and held it, so the overhead kerosene lamp shed light on the words. After reading through it once, she shook her head from side to side and reread it before asking, "Salvation through Jesus? How is that so?"

Emma took the paper from Katie's outstretched hand and placed it back in its envelope. "I'm not certain, but she wouldn't have left me a letter like that unless she was set on teaching me something."

Katie leaned in and whispered even though no one was in the room but the two of them. "Have you shown Samuel?"

"No, not yet. I wanted to try to make sense of it first."

Katie picked her coffee back up. "Your mother was quite sick that summer while you were away. Maybe she wasn't in her right mind when she wrote it."

"I'm not sure myself, I don't really understand it." Emma quickly changed the subject.

***

Daniel strolled into the barn and waved to Samuel. "Good preaching this morning, *jah*?"

Samuel latched Oliver's stall. "I wouldn't ask your *schwester* that."

Daniel propped his foot upon a rung of the gate. "Yeah, I thought she might find the message a little too close for comfort. It seems when we're struggling, the ministers have a way of saying things to convict us."

Samuel sat the horse brush on a shelf just outside the gate, "I'd say they planned all three sermons around Emma."

Daniel flipped over a five-gallon bucket to use as a stool. "She'll come around, I'm sure of it. You're talking about the girl that found out she was born English, met our birth mother, and then found out our father was Amish. After all we've been through the last few years, she's pretty tough."

Samuel took his hat off and brushed hay off his pant leg. "I thought that too, but she's pulling back pretty hard. There must be more than just losing James. Something ...but I can't seem to put my finger on it yet."

"Have you thought about taking her to Marie's?"

"It crossed my mind, but with trying to finish the house and all, I didn't think I could take the time away. I sure wish her mother, Stella, was still alive. She always knew what to say to help her come to terms with things."

Daniel picked up a piece of straw from the floor and rolled it between his fingers. "Emma hasn't known Marie but for a few years, but she is a mother, maybe she could help. They got pretty close when she stayed in Sugarcreek with her."

Samuel placed his hat back on his head. "It seems like I can't say anything right these days."

"Join the club. Katie's so cranky, it's all I can do to stay out of her way."

Samuel slapped Daniel on the shoulder. "If I had to cart around that basketball all day like she has to, I'd be ornery too."

Daniel chuckled. "It won't be too much longer. That baby should be making his way into the world any day now."

"Hoping for a boy, *jah*?"

"Don't we all?"

Samuel dropped his head and kicked a clump of mud free from his boot. "I know I did."

Daniel stood and stacked the bucket on top of another one by the wall. "The last thing you need is talk of *kinner*."

"There is no need to apologize. Life goes on, and we'll have more *kinner* one day."

Daniel walked to the large double door and pulled it open enough so they could slip through. "Come on, let's go cheer that *schwester* of mine up some."

Samuel led the way back to the house and squared his shoulders as he pushed open the door that led to the kitchen. "I hope coffee's ready. I sure could use something hot."

Emma turned and reached for the white porcelain pot as Samuel and Daniel removed their coats and boots.

Katie tried to push away the heaviness in the room. "Emma and I were just talking about the differences between men and women."

Daniel pulled a chair up next to Katie and put his arm around the back of her chair. "Now that's a topic I'd just as soon ignore. Like the plague."

"You and me both," Samuel added.

Katie reached for a cookie off the platter in the middle of the table. "Maybe we can take a walk to see the new house."

They all turned to Emma, and Samuel asked, "*Jah?*"

Emma's desire to flee outweighed the hopeful look on her husband's face as he pleaded with his eyes for her to agree.

She answered with a sigh. "Sure."

Samuel turned toward his *schwester*. "Can you walk that far?"

Katie pushed away from the table and shot her *bruder* a look. "I'm pregnant, not an invalid."

With the mention of being pregnant, all three looked in Emma's direction and held their breath.

She gestured her hand toward the door. "Go, I'm fine, and you can all stop walking on ice. I'm not going to melt."

A lightness in her tone made them all relax, and Samuel returned a slight smile in her direction.

A crispness in the air filled Emma's lungs as she walked to her new home. Maybe Samuel was right in working so hard to finish it. She couldn't help but be excited at all he'd done, and she chastised herself for not allowing herself the joy of seeing it before this. The sun was trying to make its way through a mirage of darkening clouds to shine a light on the two-story farmhouse that sat down the lane behind Levi and Ruth's farm.

Samuel positioned the front porch at such an angle that they'd be able to watch as the strawberry fields came alive with tiny white flowers in the spring. He was sure she'd be able to enjoy the sweetness through the kitchen window whenever a northwestern wind blew across the field. They planned every window and the wrap-around porch to take in as much of mother nature as possible. Samuel even went as far as to keep in mind the angle of the sun in relationship to the garden, so she wouldn't struggle when it came time to plant.

He took great care in building their new home, and she again scolded herself for not showing any interest in his hard work. They walked down the lane slowly as Katie struggled to keep her balance on the icy lane. Daniel held her elbow and guided each step of their way. Samuel looked over to her and smiled tenderly as Katie reprimanded Daniel for coddling her.

Samuel reached down and took Emma's gloved hand and squeezed it ever so lightly. There was a warmth in his touch she couldn't deny, no matter how hard she tried. After everything they'd been through, she treasured the moment before reality came crashing down on her once again.

Samuel dropped her hand and rushed ahead to help Daniel guide his *schwester* up the stairs. "Would you two stop? I'm plenty capable of walking up a few steps."

In unison they said, "They're icy."

Both men took an arm and guided her up the stairs one step at a time. Samuel looked back to Emma and hollered, "Wait! I'll be back for you."

She knew exactly what all the fuss was about and didn't dare proceed without her husband's arm to lean on.

Once Katie was safely inside, Samuel rushed to her side, placed his hand under her elbow, and steadied her up the slippery steps. "Had I known we were coming today, I would have shoveled and salted the walkway."

Emma stopped before they got to the door and pulled him toward her. "It was an accident."

He turned toward her voice. "One that was preventable if I wouldn't have been in such a hurry."

She saw the regret in his eyes that spoke of the pain, much louder than she'd ever noticed before. "I don't blame you."

He pulled her close, and she melted into his chest, letting so much of their hurt blend together as one. He rested his chin on top of her brown bonnet and slowly swayed back and forth and muttered, "His ways are not for us to understand but accept."

Her back stiffened, and she pulled away from his embrace and uttered, "I won't."

She stepped through the door and tried to smile as Katie oohed and ahhed over the polished pine floors. The tender moment they shared before stepping inside was soon a thing of the past as hostility made its way back to the present.

Katie and Daniel, oblivious to her change in demeanor, made their way to the kitchen to admire the cabinets her father made for them. She stayed back and let the empty room remind her there would be no children to run up and down the stairs, no babies to rock to sleep, and no games of checkers in front of the fireplace.

Daniel and Samuel ran their hands over the countertops and explained to Katie the trials they had installing them. Katie's excitement made up for her sudden lack of interest, and she quietly made her way upstairs. At the top of the stairs, she stopped and contemplated which room she wanted to visit first. Two on one side of the hall and three on the other. The first room was the largest of them all, with a small alcove set off to the side that would act as a nursery.

They planned this room especially for their early years when they could keep the littlest of their children close by. When she walked through the door that led to the pale-yellow painted room attached to the master bedroom, she let a ray of sunshine lead her to the window. Staring out over the barren strawberry fields covered in snow, she remembered how they had planned the room, so she could always see Samuel work as she tended to their children.

Moving from their bedroom, she made her way past each room until stopping at the end of the hall. Surprised to find the door locked, she slid her hand over the top of the door frame until her fingers found the key. She furrowed her eyebrows as curiosity forced her to turn the knob against the key.

Light filtered in through the curtainless windows, and her eyes adjusted to the blaring sun. In the center of the room, a braided blue and yellow rug held a rocking chair, James' baby cradle, and a little windup swing to lure him to sleep when she couldn't. Before that moment, she hadn't given the furniture another thought. The rug made a beautiful backdrop to the matching oak chair and cradle, and she crumpled to the floor in front of each. Beside her was a box of baby clothes and brand-new cloth diapers. Everything was waiting in vain. The realization that his little feet or bare bottom would never touch the items in the box was unbearable.

Her husband's voice bounced off the hallway walls.

"Emma?"

The pain in his tone magnified as he knelt beside her. "I locked these things in here so you wouldn't have to face them. I'm sorry, I should have hidden them in the barn."

He wrapped his arms around her. When she leaned into his shoulder, she saw Katie in the doorway. The pity engraved on her face was more than she could stand. She lashed out. "Go! It's not fair." She buried her head in Samuel's shoulder and sobbed. "Please, Daniel, take her home."

CHAPTER 5

K atie rolled to her side and curled up close to Daniel's back, letting the weight of her middle rest in the crook of his spine. Resting her arm across his hip, she snuggled in closer when a deep approving moan escaped his slumber.

For two hours, Katie struggled to find relief from the ache in her lower back. With the restlessness of the child moving inside of her, she let Daniel carry the heaviness of them both when her belly rested against his back.

Without rolling over, he held her hand. "How's my girl this morning?"

"A little achy."

"Anything we need to be concerned with?"

"I'm sure he's just getting anxious to meet his *datt* and is trying to tell me he's had enough of this cocoon."

"How about I go make you breakfast in bed?"

"I don't feel much like eating yet, and besides, that's my job, not yours. What would the bishop think if he found out you were doing woman's work?"

Daniel rolled to his back and moved his arm under Katie's head so she could rest on his shoulder. "I don't care what he or anyone else might think. There is nothing wrong with taking some of my wife's load."

Katie laid her hand on his chest. "I don't think carrying your child is a burden at all. I'm quite fond of a part of you growing inside of me. But I have to say I'd appreciate it if I'd stop getting so big. Not so sure how much more my tiny frame can hold."

He kissed the top of her head. "Not much longer, my love."

"*Nee*, just a couple of weeks and hopefully in time for Christmas."

She closed her eyes and savored the tranquil moment of her husband's heartbeat in her ear. His breath deepened, and a slight snore escaped his lips.

Sleep didn't come for her as she replayed yesterday's explosion with Emma in her head. Her best friend was hurting, and there was nothing she could do or say to help her through this bleak moment. She held no anger toward Emma and silently prayed *God* would reach her friend.

Lord,

I trust you have a purpose in all you do. Please help Emma see that You work all things for the good of those who love you. She's lost and hurting, please my Lord, surround her with a wedge of protection and pull her through this most trying time.

Your will be done, Amen

***

The sky, heavy with clouds and slivers of orange and yellow trying to make their way through the sunrise, greeted Samuel on the porch of the *doddi haus*. One step forward and two steps back was all he could think about. For a short period yesterday, he saw glimpses of Emma returning. Still, after her meltdown, there was no light through the darkness that surrounded her.

At his wit's end, he made the decision to call her birth mother in Sugarcreek. His mother mentioned Marie called the other day, and as far as he could tell, Emma had yet to return her call. Nothing he said or did made any headway, and he prayed his mother-in-law would be willing to give it a try.

The short walk to the phone shanty at the end of the lane helped clear his head and figure out how much he would share with Marie. He couldn't help but think he was betraying Emma by asking Marie for help. His mother-in-law had a young family of her own. Was he asking too much to add one more burden to her already full plate? But again, he had tried everything. Who else could he turn to?

Pulling the door closed, he dialed the number to Marie's husband's business and held his breath as the phone rang on the other end.

"Bouteright Stables, Nathan here."

"Nathan, it's Samuel, Samuel Yoder, Emma's husband."

"Samuel, sorry about your son."

"*Denki.*"

"Death is never an easy thing to work through. And Emma, how is she doing?"

"Not good." Samuel cleared his throat. "I'm hoping Marie might be able to help."

"Not sure what she can do two hours away, but she'll do whatever you need. I know she tried to call the other day. Did Emma receive the message?"

"I'm certain of it, but she's not in her right mind lately. I've not been able to get through to her and neither has anyone else around here. We've tried. Even some of the women in the community have reached out to her, but she's shut everyone out."

Nathan paused before asking, "You think Marie can help?"

"I'm not sure, but she's my last hope."

Nathan pushed the silence to an uncomfortable limit. "Sometimes the only thing that helps is time."

"*Jah.*"

"Give her time to work through it, but in the meantime, I'm sure Marie would enjoy a visit from Emma."

"*Denki*, I'll hire a driver today."

Samuel didn't wait for Nathan to say goodbye before he disconnected the call. His father-in-law's advice to give her more time fell on deaf ears as he dialed his English driver's number.

***

Emma pulled the quilt over her head when Samuel's heavy boots made their way up the stairs and into their room. The shade slapped against the window just before the mattress shifted under his weight.

"Emma, I know you're awake. I heard you in the bathroom a few minutes ago."

There was no denying his presence, but he'd have to do so behind the darkness of her blanket.

"What do you want?"

"First uncover your head and talk to me." He pulled the quilt away from her face, but she tightened her hold on the fabric and curled into a fetal position.

"Later."

He yanked the bedding from her fingertips, forcing her to face him. She threw her arm over her eyes to shield the morning light spilling into the room.

"What is it? I'm in no mood to deal with you today."

"Regardless, you need to get up and pack a bag. A driver will be here within the hour to take you to Sugarcreek."

"I have no plans to go anywhere today."

"You do now. Your mother is expecting you."

She turned on her side away from him and grabbed the edge of the quilt, pulling it over her bare legs.

"It's time to come back to the real world and find a way to deal with all of this. Maybe your mother will have better luck than me."

He tore the blanket from the bed and tossed it on the floor. "It's one thing to suffer and mourn, but another when you lash out at those who love you. There was no excuse for the way you treated Daniel and Katie yesterday. Some time away is exactly what you need."

"I'll apologize to them if that's what you want, but I'm not going to my mother's."

He walked to the small dresser across the room and pulled items from the drawer. "As I said, you don't have much say in the matter. I've already made plans, and your mother is expecting you."

Emma sat up in bed and pulled her knees to her chest locking them in with her long white nightdress. "So, you're shipping me away just like that? The first real struggle we face, and you pawn me off on someone else? Not the best decision you've made as head of our household."

She waited to gauge his reaction before she continued. "Did the bishop put you up to this?"

He dropped to his knees and pulled a small brown leather suitcase out from under the bed. "The bishop doesn't advise me on all things, and certainly not on my choice to send you to your mother's for a few days."

The stack of clothes he threw on the bed sat in a jumbled mess, and he pushed them aside to open the suitcase. "I don't know what else to do. I've sympathized with you, prayed for you, held you, even begged my mother and Katie to help ...and nothing. You're not getting any better."

In not much more than a whisper, she begged. "Please don't send me away. I just need time."

He sat on the edge of the bed, rested his elbows on his knees, and clasped his hands. "Six weeks is more than enough time to move on. God's will is done ...life goes on. We have a house to finish, the bakery to open, and more children to plan for. What's done is done."

Without looking back at her, he moved to the door. "I'll wait for you downstairs."

The harshness in his voice was alarming. There was no doubt he had lost his patience, and all she could do was comply.

With a heavy heart, she dressed then carried the bag to the bottom of the stairs.

Samuel sat in his chair at the head of the table, looking through his wallet. "Funds are tight at the moment, but this should be plenty to pay the driver when you're ready to come home."

"If we can't afford it, then let me stay."

"I've already made my decision. I think you need time away."

It took all she had to reach up and lay her hand across the back of his forearm. "Or do you need time away from me?"

Tires crunching on the frozen driveway alerted them long before the driver blew the horn. He patted the back of her hand. "I'll see you in a few days, *jah*?"

An overwhelming sadness filled her soul as she walked to the door without Samuel following her. She didn't look back and he didn't move from his chair. How could he send her away when he was the one thing, she needed the most? Maybe he was right. A few days away to help her figure out how to tell him there may be no more children for them is just what she needed.

***

The streetlights lining Main Street in Willow Springs were dressed for the holidays and quickly reminded Emma that Christmas was only two weeks away. The first of many events and holidays they would celebrate without James. Every minute of every day was etched in and around the baby boy she longed to hold.

The two-hour car ride to Marie's did little to calm her racing pulse. Even though the driver did his best to pull her into a comfortable conversation, her one-word answers finally deterred him from trying.

She leaned her forehead against the side of the cold window pane and closed her eyes and thought. *Why God? Why my baby?* The warm car and the steady motion made her sleepy, and she gave in to the heaviness behind her eyes.

***

"Emma, we're here."

Caught somewhere between a dream and reality, Emma heard her name being called but fought to stay in a dream like state, singing her baby to sleep.

"Emma, you can wake up now. We made it to Bouteright Stables."

Like water running through her fingers, she felt the small child slip away from her once again. Trying to hold on for a few more moments, she resisted opening her eyes until the driver's voice called to her again.

"Emma, wake up."

She slipped her arms in the sleeves of her coat and looked out the window. Nathan and Marie's home looked the same as it had three years prior. The well-manicured house and stables were a picture of Nathan's success, and she instantly felt at ease.

Marie and Nathan married three years earlier and had already added baby Lydia and Nathaniel Jr. to their growing family. In her mother's letters, she learned Amos and Rachel enjoyed their big brother and big sister roles. Nathan's first wife was killed in a buggy accident, and Marie warmly accepted his *kinner* as her own.

Marie waved her in as she bounced eighteen-month-old Lydia on her hip. A pang of apprehension filled Emma's stomach as she thought about seeing six-month-old Nathaniel. It was too late to turn back now, and if this was what Samuel thought she needed, she would at least entertain his request for a few days.

Marie met her at the base of the stairs and hugged her with her free arm. "I'm so sorry I couldn't come to Willow Springs. Things are so busy at the stables, and Nathan's mother Rosie isn't well these days. To say the least, my days are quite busy."

"Momma, no need to apologize. You have a family to take care of. The last thing you need to worry about is me. Besides, nothing a few days in your busy house won't cure. I'm certain of it."

Marie let a small giggle work in the back of her throat before she replied. "Let's see how you feel after you spend a few sleepless nights listening to my cranky baby."

Her mother wrapped her arm around her shoulders and led her into the kitchen. "Please excuse the mess. I was in the middle of making dinner when Lydia pulled my apron full of eggs off the table. You'd think I'd know better than to leave the string hanging down where she could reach it. It was all I could do to gather eggs; let alone put them away. They are so few and far between this time of year, it made me sick they got wasted."

Emma took her coat off and set her suitcase at her feet. "Here, let me help." She carried the trash can to the table and scooped the runny eggs up off the floor with her hands. Falling right in step with her mother, she helped Marie put dinner on the table, Lydia fed, and Rosie tended to, all before Nathan came in from the stables.

Once they all bowed their heads in silent prayer, Nathan tapped his fork on the side of his plate, and both women lifted their heads. Marie sat back in her chair and let out a slow breath and relaxed her shoulders. "I forgot how smoothly this house runs when Emma's here."

Nathan buttered a slice of bread and dipped it in his stew. "I bet she won't miss the craziness when all the farmhands show up for supper later. We got a reprieve for dinner. I sent them all into town to pick up a big order of fencing supplies."

Marie reached her hand over and patted her daughter's arm. "How are you? Samuel says you've been struggling."

Emma pushed the meat and vegetables around on her plate. "I suppose not any worse than any other mother who loses a child."

Marie held up a finger before she had a chance to elaborate on what she was dealing with. "Hold that thought. I'll be right back."

Nathan tipped his head in the direction of the stairs. "Sounds like Jr. up there has plans to keep his *mamm* away from enjoying a hot meal."

Emma took the napkin off her lap and held her hand out to stop her mother from leaving the table. "Stay, enjoy your dinner."

"Are you sure? You're supposed to be here relaxing, not taking care of my children."

Emma followed the baby's cry up the stairs as her mother hollered after her. "I just fed him, so he probably has a bubble."

Her heart pounded in fear with every step she took closer to the wailing child. Would she be able to comfort the child without turning into a blubbering mess? This certainly would be a test she wasn't so sure she could pass.

Emma slowly opened the door to find the little one had pushed himself up in the corner of the cradle, struggling to find his thumb. Her motherly instinct took over, and she rolled him to his back, swaddled him in a blanket, and settled into the rocking chair near the window. He promptly settled down when she set the chair in motion and rubbed tiny circles between his shoulder blades. Dark wisps of hair tickled her nose, and she took in the fresh baby scent as she buried her cheek in the back of his head. He cooed and squirmed until he found his thumb and went back to sleep.

A fresh set of tears landed on top of his tiny head. She let just a few fall before she tucked them back away, hidden in her own grief.

The sun coming in through the window lured her back to sleep as she held her mother's child close to her heart. It was not until she felt Marie lift the boy from her arms, did she stir.

"I'm sorry. I fell asleep."

"I hated to wake you, but Amos and Rachel are biting at the bit."

Tucking the baby back into the cradle, Marie held her finger to her lips as she motioned for Emma to follow her back downstairs. Only after she quietly closed the door did she explain. "School has parent-teacher meetings this afternoon, so Amos and Rachel only had a half-day of school. They're downstairs having a snack."

She couldn't deny she was excited to visit with Nathan's children. They both ran to her the minute she made it to the bottom of the stairs. "Hold on there, you about knocked me over."

Rachel wrapped her arms around her middle, and Amos pushed his *schwester* aside for a tighter grip. "Let me look at you. You've both grown so much I hardly recognize you."

Amos stood up tall. "I'm seven now, and I come up to *datt's* chest. I'll be as tall as him someday."

Emma patted the top of his head. "I'm sure you will." She pushed Rachel back for a closer look. "Look at you. You're not a little girl anymore. Before long, you'll be going to *singeons* and snagging every boy in the community."

"I'm only ten. Way too young to go to a youth gathering."

"Ten, wow! You look so much older. I'd better have a talk with Marie and tell her to stop making you drink so much milk."

They all giggled and headed back to the table. Emma sat between them, and Lydia held her hands out, begging to be picked up.

Marie picked up a dishcloth and wiped crumbs off Lydia's highchair. "No other word but crazy to describe what goes on around here. I never dreamed four kids would be so much work! Doesn't help I'm in my forties. Most women my age are done with babies by now."

Emma twisted her head until she caught her mother's eye. "Do you regret it?"

"Not for one minute. Days of regretting things I have no control over are long gone. The Lord gave me something I thought I had lost forever. Love, family, and children. What more could a mother ask for?"

No sooner did the words leave her mouth than Marie held her hand to her lips and whispered, "I'm sorry."

CHAPTER 6

Four days had passed since Emma arrived at Marie and Nathan's, and she had yet to get a chance to speak with her mother. The few minutes she did have between spilled milk and making meals was spent helping with the children. There was no doubt Marie had her hands full and the last thing her mother needed was to have her cry on her shoulder. What she did have time for was spending quality time with Rosie. The old woman was wise beyond her years, and Emma took every opportunity to be in her presence.

Crippled with rheumatoid arthritis, Rosie was confined to bed and struggled with a dry cough and shortness of breath. Even the slightest excitement left her in a weakened state.

Emma lightly knocked on Rosie's door before pushing it open to carry her breakfast tray to her bedside.

In not much more than a whisper Emma asked, "Rosie, are you awake? I've brought you some oatmeal and a cup of your favorite tea."

Rosie tilted her head in Emma's direction and pointed to the chair near the bed. "Bless ...you."

Emma set the tray down and carried the steaming cup to her side. "I heard you coughing. How about you take a few sips of tea? I added extra honey to help soothe your throat."

Rosie's distorted fingers grasped the cup, and it splashed over the side as she brought it to her mouth.

Emma moved closer. "Here, let me help."

The lines stamped in the corners of the old woman's eyes were moist, and Emma tried to ease her frustration. "No shame in needing help."

Rosie leaned in and dropped her hands to her lap as Emma held the cup to her lips. Once she had her fill, she rested her head back on the pillows Emma had stacked up around her and asked through a ragged wheeze, "Tell me ...about ...him."

"Who?"

"Your ...baby."

Emma's heart quickened. "You want to know about James?"

"*Jah* ...tell me ...everything."

She sniffled and reached for Rosie's hand. "No one's ever asked to hear about him before."

"His hair ...what ...color?"

Emma gave a slight smile and tilted her head and closed her eyes. "His head was covered in soft wisps of baby fuzz. I remember laying my lips against his head, and the fine hair tickled my nose."

"How ...much...did he weigh?"

"He was born almost two months early, so he was tiny. Just four pounds."

"And ... his eyes?"

Emma pulled her hand from Rosie's and turned to gather the tray. "I didn't see his eyes."

Rosie reached and tried to grab her sleeve. "No ...don't go."

"I should let you rest."

"I can rest ...later ...pleeasse...stay."

Emma's thoughts suddenly became dull, and a rush of emotion filled her head as if a tornado had cleared a path through her heart.

Rosie's disfigured fingers tugged at the fabric of Emma's apron. "You ...know Jesus, *jah*?"

That one question had haunted her for a week or so, and it still held a void in her mind. Did she know Jesus? Is that what Stella was trying to show her? If she did, she surely couldn't feel his presence in her life or understand what it meant.

The desperation in Rosie's voice left her no option but to pacify the woman's plea. "*Jah,* I know of Jesus."

She left the tray and headed to the door.

Without an ounce of rattle in the aging woman's voice, Rosie said, "You're not alone. He's waiting for you to call His name."

She stopped in her tracks and turned in anticipation of seeing Rosie's stare, but instead, she found the old woman's head relaxed on the pillow, drifting off to sleep.

There was a calmness in the room that enticed her to stay. Even the goosebumps forming at the base of her neck wouldn't explain her sudden urge to sink to the floor.

A cry from the other room forced her to turn back to the door but not before she noticed a spectrum of colors bouncing off Rosie's glass, making a beautiful show on the wall. In an instant, she was taken back to sitting on her father's knee as they marveled at a rainbow. The memory was as vivid as the kaleidoscope of colors leaping through the air. She couldn't have been more than six when her *datt* pointed to the sky and whispered in her ear. "Remember, every time you see a rainbow - God is telling you He will always keep His promises."

She wasn't sure she knew what he meant then and wasn't sure she understood its significance now, but the whole scene left her speechless. She had so many questions but didn't know where to turn for the answers.

"Emma! Can you give me a hand?"

Marie's voice beckoned her to the kitchen, and she forced herself to push the memory away until later.

Lydia cried to get out of her highchair while Marie changed the baby on the daybed set up in the corner of the room.

Emma unlocked the tray and picked Lydia up from her seat. Carrying her to the sink to wipe the jelly from her hands, she cooed soothing sounds in the little girl's ear.

"There, there, little one, let's dry up those tears."

As if there was someone over her shoulder, her own words echoed in her ear, *there, there little one, let's dry up those tears.* She quickly turned toward the voice but met nothing but emptiness.

Marie propped Nathaniel over her shoulder and met Emma at the sink. "We haven't had two minutes to ourselves since you walked in the door, but have I told you what a blessing you've been to me the last few days?"

"It's the least I could do since you agreed to let me visit on such short notice. Being busy like this has done more than you can imagine."

"Let's get these two down for a nap, and we can visit some before Nathan and his crew come in for dinner."

Marie balanced both children on her hip and headed up the stairs. "I'll be right back."

Emma moved to the living room and sat in one of the two rockers that faced the front window. She laid her head back and set the chair in motion with her foot. With her eyes closed, she tried to remember exactly what Rosie had said. *He is waiting for you to call His name.* A slight ache deep behind the small incision in her lower abdomen reminded her she probably shouldn't be toting Lydia around. Rubbing small circles around the painful reminder, she thought, *do I know Jesus?* She spoke out loud, "What does that mean?"

Marie laid her hand on her shoulder. "What does what mean?"

Emma reached up and covered her hand with her own. "It's not important."

Marie pulled the chair closer and leaned into Emma. "Talk to me. What's going through that pretty little head of yours?"

"Half my problem is that I can't make much sense of anything these days."

"My heart aches for you, and I wish I knew the words to help you through this. Maybe you need to talk to someone."

"You know as well as I do; it's not our way."

"Maybe not your ways, but you have to remember I've only been Amish for a few years. In the English world, counselors can do a great deal of good. Nathan's district is a little more progressive than yours. Perhaps I can talk to him about finding someone for you."

"Samuel would never allow it."

"I think you're wrong about that. Samuel is at the end of his rope, and I'm sure if he knew how much they could help, he'd agree."

Emma played with a string on the hem of her sleeve. "Maybe so, but I'm not sure that's the answer for what's bothering me most."

"How about you tell me what's troubling you, besides the obvious."

Emma tipped her head back and closed her eyes again. "I think God is punishing us."

Marie furrowed her eyebrows. "God doesn't punish like that. He might use our struggles to teach us something, much like a mother teaches a child, but He doesn't punish us the way you think."

"But He took James, and I may not be able to have more children. That sure seems like a punishment to me."

"What on earth are you talking about? What happened to you was an accident, and no reason you can't conceive again."

Emma grasped the arms of the chair. "You don't understand."

Marie patted her knee. "I don't think I do. What is it?"

"I can't get pregnant for two years, or I'll risk the chance of putting another baby in danger."

"I don't understand the issue in waiting a couple of years to have another child."

Free-flowing tears met Emma's chin. "Momma, I can't deny Samuel and, our marriage bed for ...*two years*."

"Is that what you're so distraught about?"

"I must have done something to God for him to do this to me. How can I put my trust in a God who would take a child from a loving mother's arms?"

Marie moved her chair closer. "We must believe He has a plan in everything He does, and it isn't your fault. This was an accident and God's will."

Marie picked up the bible from the stand between the two chairs. "I have something for you." She opened the brown leather-lined book to a flowery piece of cardstock tucked between some pages. "Do you remember when I found this in my mother's bible? It was a turning point in my life, and you were right there with me."

Emma took the bookmark from her mother's hand and focused on the words through cloudy eyes. IF YOU SENSE YOUR FAITH IS UNRAVELLING, GO BACK TO WHERE YOU DROPPED THE THREAD OF OBEDIENCE. She handed it back to her mother.

"No, I want you to keep it. If I remember correctly, it was you who asked me how I couldn't see God's hand in my life a few years ago. Now I'm asking you the same. How can you think God doesn't have a hand in this? He orchestrates all things for His good. You told me that, remember? Now, it's time you go back and pick up that thread of obedience. You are doubting God's hand in all of this and all He asks us to do is trust Him and be obedient. We aren't called to understand everything He does, but to have faith to know He sees things we can't. He wants you to be the woman who trusts and says yes to all He asks of you. Which includes accepting this path and moving on."

Marie laid the bible on Emma's lap. "I think you can find a lot of comfort in here."

"I can't take that; we are instructed to read from our German Martin Luther Bible."

"Right now, you're in my house, and around here, we read from the English Bible, and besides, how much of that German version do you understand?"

"Not much."

"That's what I thought. Look, I realize your Old Order community is different from our New Order, but maybe it wouldn't hurt for you to read the Lord's words for yourself. You need to learn the truth and understand how He sent His son to die for us so we could live a life without pain and sorrow."

"How can that be? All that's in front of me right now is pain and sorrow."

Marie patted the leather cover of her mother's old bible. "All your answers are in here. Read it, you'll learn this heartache is only temporary. God has so much more planned for you. He has a purpose for your life and I'm certain losing James has something to do with it."

"How can you be so sure?"

"Because I lost you for sixteen years and look what I've gained through all of my troubles. If it wasn't for you forgiving me and showing me how important God was in your life. I wouldn't be where I'm at today."

Marie crossed her legs and leaned closer to Emma. "You're just temporarily lost and confused. You thought you knew God before, but I can guarantee you if you read His word, you'll soon discover a God bigger and better than anything you could imagine. I have a feeling this is His way of leading you into a deeper relationship with Him."

Emma outlined the leather cover with her finger. "Stella left me a letter where she encouraged me to look for the truth in Jesus. What you're describing is much like what she said."

"Now if both of your mother's are saying the same thing, don't you think that's something pretty important?"

Emma rubbed her temples and closed her eyes. "I'm still so angry I don't even know where to start to open my heart back up."

Marie tapped the Bible on Emma's lap. "Start here. Then tell Samuel what the doctor advised."

"But he'll be so disappointed."

Marie leaned back in her chair. "Don't you think you need to discuss it with him before you make any harsh conclusions as to what or how he will think?"

"But I can't risk the life of another child."

"Emma, you're not thinking rationally. You need to talk to Samuel like you should have done the minute you found out. Don't you think he has the right to understand what's really bothering you?"

Emma dropped her head and wiped a lingering tear from her cheek. "I suppose."

Marie laid her hand on Emma's knee. "I'd say it's time to go home."

***

Nathan hired a driver to take her back to Willow Springs. The driver, Frank sat patiently in the driveway while she said her goodbyes. It was already late in the day, but Emma wanted to wait until the children came home from school before leaving.

Marie held her close. "Take one day at a time and remember when we walk through trials, He is right there walking them with us if we allow it."

Her mother's hug did little to calm the rolling waves of anxiousness rooted deep inside. "I'll try."

Marie pushed back and tenderly tucked a wisp of Emma's hair under her heavy brown bonnet. "You'll tell Samuel what the doctors advised ...right?"

"*Jah*"

"That's my girl. Now go home to him. I'm sure he's missing you."

Emma picked up her bag and slid into the backseat just as a gust of wind blew through the open door.

Frank turned in his seat. "Looks like a storm's brewing. We best get on the road."

Emma waved at Marie and buckled the belt around her heavy wool coat. "I'd like to make one quick stop before we head out. Do you know where the Shetler farm is?"

"Lillian Shetler?"

"Yes. I'd like to stop and say a quick hello to my grandmother before I leave town."

The driver pulled out into the road. "By the looks of those clouds, I'd say it best be speedy. I'd hate to be stuck on the Turnpike in the storm blowing across Lake Erie."

"I promise I'll make it quick."

Emma sat back and wished she'd found time to visit with *Mommi* Lillian earlier. The long driveway that led to her grandparent's farm was covered in snow with little signs of life. Only a single pair of footprints led from the house to the dairy barn across the yard.

The driver leaned over the steering wheel for a better look at the looming sky. "You've got about ten minutes before we have to get on the road."

"I'll hurry." Emma ran up the stairs and knocked, hoping it wouldn't take her grandmother long to answer. After a few seconds, she rapped a little louder and called out *Mommi* Lillian's name.

A bellowing voice rang out behind her. "She's not home."

Her Uncle Jay walked across the yard, flipping his collar up to block the wind. "Nobody here but me. *Mamm's* visiting her *schwester* in Pinecraft."

Emma wrapped her arms around her middle and walked down the steps. The ache in her heart filled with regret. "How long is she staying?"

"Can't say. *Mamm* said she wasn't coming back until the Robins returned."

Emma snickered. "That won't be for at least three or four months."

"Suppose so."

Jay was a man of few words, plus Emma hadn't said more than a handful of words to him in the three years she'd known him. An uncomfortable silence bounced between them. "Well, if you hear from her, please tell her I stopped by."

Jay nodded his head, and Emma climbed back into the warm car. "I guess we can be on our way now."

Emma settled in for the two-hour ride home. In the back of her mind, she hoped she could talk Lillian into allowing her to stay a few days longer. Her mother meant well, but Emma wasn't ready to go home just yet. Samuel was too quick to send her away, and she wasn't prepared to face the hopelessness that awaited her there.

Frank slowed down at the bend in the road in front of the Sugarcreek Auction house. "I need to make one quick stop at the Bulk Foods Store up here on the right. If you want to grab a drink and a snack, now's the time. I won't be stopping again before we make it to Willow Springs."

"Thanks, I might just do that."

The parking lot was bustling, and a large coach bus sat at the curb. She followed Frank to the front of the store. A poster advertising Sarasota, Florida, took up much of the window as the driver held the door.

"Looks like another load of snowbirds going to Florida," he mentioned.

Emma stopped and looked back outside. Older couples were leaving their suitcases on the curb and rushing onboard and out of the whistling wind. "I forgot my money, is the car unlocked?"

"Sure is. I'll meet you back at the car in about ten minutes."

Two women stood in the line loading the bus when she headed back outside. It was hard not to overhear their conversation.

One woman shook her head from side to side. "Such a shame Ella's not feeling well, it's a shame her ticket will go to waste."

CHAPTER 7

Samuel glanced at the clock when it rang seven chimes. A northeastern gust blew around the house, and he was worried Emma might be caught in the storm. He wouldn't relax until she was safely back home.

It was less than a week until Christmas, and he was excited to tell her they could finally move into their new house. He'd spent the last five days working long hours finishing everything up. Hopefully, the time away gave her a new sense of purpose, and she'd be ready to move on with life.

Stacking a few dishes in the sink, he peered out the window, hoping the lights of a car would pull in the driveway. He pulled a chair close to the window in the front room. After two hours, he put on his coat and boots and headed out to the phone shanty. Maybe the weather-delayed her, and she left a message for him there.

The light on the machine blinked green, and he pressed the play button. He quickly deleted it, realizing he forgot to delete Nathan's earlier message telling him Emma was on her way home. When no other call was recorded, he dialed Bouteright Stables.

After a few rings, Nathan's answering machine picked up and he left a message. "Nathan, Emma's not made it home yet. I wondered if you received any word from the driver." He paused for a moment before continuing. "A storm blew in early this evening. Maybe they got delayed? If you hear any word from the driver, can you call me back?"

After hanging up, he let his headlamp recoil a warm glow on the pine plank walls. He dropped his head and said a silent prayer for Emma's protection.

Samuel checked the phone shanty for messages on the hour, every hour, for the next twenty-four hours. As morning light eased its way over the horizon, an uneasy dread settled between his shoulder blades. It was time he told his parents, along with Emma's father, she was missing. He retrieved Nathan's message explaining his hired driver stopped at a store before they headed out. When he came back to the car, she was gone. He waited for over an hour, but when she didn't return, he assumed she changed her mind about going to Pennsylvania.

He pushed open the door to the small wooden shed at the end of the lane and shielded his eyes from the sun glaring off the white-covered ground. The storm dropped a foot of new snow he had to kick away from the door before opening it. The clip-clop of a horse and buggy stopped short of where he stood. Samuel walked to its side and waited for Daniel to pull the brown canvas covering the door back.

"I'd say that long face has something to do with Emma not being back yet."

Samuel moved closer. "Much worse."

"How much worse can it be than my sister leaving my best friend to fend for himself?"

"I can't find her."

"What do you mean you can't find her? How did you lose your wife?"

"She was supposed to be home yesterday. Nathan left a message saying she was on her way, and I waited up all night and nothing. He even tracked down her driver who said she ditched him at some bulk food store in Sugarcreek."

Daniel raised one eyebrow. "The bulk store near the auction house?"

"I have no idea. The driver said he went in for a drink, and when he came out, she was gone."

"What time was it when they left?"

Samuel's eyes fixed on the frozen ground. "I think Nathan said she left around three or so."

Daniel's lip twitched. "That sister of mine went to Florida."

"Florida? Why on earth would you think that?"

"Because that store is where the bus line picks people up to go south to Florida. If I remember correctly; it departs in the afternoon. I bet she found a way on that bus, and she's already on her way to Sarasota."

"By herself? I can't imagine her going all the way to Florida alone. And besides, I didn't give her enough money for a bus ticket. Let alone lodging."

Daniel snickered. "I know it's not funny, but you have to agree when Emma wants something bad enough, she usually finds a way to get it."

"But Florida? She doesn't even know anyone there."

"She's been pretty depressed the last couple of months. Maybe some warm sunshine is just what she needs."

Samuel kicked an ice mound with the toe of his boot. "I swear that woman is going to get the best of me. How on earth can I help her if I can't even find her?"

"Well, my friend, maybe you need to go after her. A woman wants to feel like she's wanted, and the way you pawned her off on Marie might have left her unwilling to come home."

"I didn't pawn her off!"

"*Nee*? Looks that way to me."

Daniel clicked his tongue to set the horse in motion and hollered over his shoulder. "I think a little sun and sand will do you both some good."

Over the metal wheels crunching snow, Samuel shouted, "But Florida, of all places? I have work to do. I can't take time chasing her all over the country!"

Daniel yelled, "Go get her!"

***

Emma took the ticket from the woman's hand. "Are you sure?"

"*Jah*, maybe the good Lord figured you needed a trip to Florida more than Ella."

Excitement filled Emma as she rushed back to the car to retrieve her suitcase. Everything was happening so fast. Maybe that was good since she didn't have time for second thoughts.

"Let me pay you for it. I don't think I have enough to cover the cost, but I can give you the rest when I get to *Mommi* Lillian's. I'm sure she won't mind giving me a short loan."

"You're Lillian Shetler's granddaughter?"

"I am. How do you know my grandmother?"

"We aren't in the same district, but we quilt together once a month. You wouldn't happen to be Emma from Willow Springs, would you?"

"I am. How do you know about me?" Emma asked.

"Lillian told us all about you and your baby."

The other woman laid her hand on her arm. "It's settled. You'll sit with us, and we won't accept any money for your ticket. It was just going to go to waste anyways with Ella getting sick and all."

Both women grabbed an arm and led her to the bus. "Leave your suitcase on the curb. The driver will put it in the undercarriage."

Emma stopped just before stepping on the bus. "I'm not sure. Maybe I ought to call home first. They're expecting me."

"No time now; the bus is due to leave any minute. You'll have plenty of time to phone home once we reach Pinecraft."

Emma turned back toward the door hoping Frank would come out of the store so she could tell him what she was doing. Hopefully, he would figure it out when she was nowhere to be found.

There was no turning back now. The driver reached for her ticket, then shut the door behind her. Following the two wider women to the middle of the bus, she sat where the first woman pointed. "Here, sit on the aisle seat so you'll be in the middle of us."

Emma sat down and took a deep breath. The bus pulled out of the parking lot just as Frank exited the store. She leaned over the woman by the window, waving to the driver, hoping he saw her on the bus. "I think I should have told my driver at least."

The larger of the two women snickered. "I'm sure he'll figure it out quick enough."

For the next hour, the two women chatted back and forth. At the same time, regret and fear mingled together with anticipation as Emma tried to relax. Finally, she interrupted her seatmates. "I didn't even catch your names."

"Oh my goodness, you're right; we never introduced ourselves. I'm Margaret Troyer."

"And I'm Betty Mullet."

Emma reached out to shake their hands. "So nice to meet you and thank you so much for sharing your ticket with me."

Margaret tucked her purse in the pocket of the seat in front of her. "It's the least we can do for Lillian's granddaughter. She would do the same for us. I'm sure of it."

Betty pulled down the armrest and tilted in Emma's direction. "So, won't Lillian be surprised when we get off the bus in Pinecraft together? She'll be in heaven for sure and certain."

Emma wrung her hands together on her lap. "I sure hope so because my husband's not going to be happy with me."

Betty murmured, "No worries, you'll be able to borrow someone's cell phone as soon as we arrive in Pinecraft. We indulge in such things down there."

Margaret leaned over and gave Betty an alarmed look. "Now Betty, you know what happens in Pinecraft stays in Pinecraft. Those things are best kept quiet." She smiled and then turned to Emma, and whispered, "You're in for quite a treat."

Margaret sat back in her chair. "Might be just what you need to wash those baby blues away."

Emma slipped her arms out of her jacket and pushed the wrinkles out of her black dress. "What makes you think I have the baby blues?"

Margaret patted her knee. "The eyes are the path to your soul, and those dark circles say more than you think. Nothing a few days in the sand and sun won't cure."

"I've never been to the beach."

Betty twisted in her seat. "What? You've never been to the beach? You must go and let all your cares wash out into the ocean."

Margaret added, "You need to go to Siesta Key. The bluish-green water meets the sky and paints a picture that will warm even the saddest soul."

"Oh, it sounds perfect."

Betty tried to cross her leg but gave up when the seat in front of her had already reclined. "We encouraged Lillian to go after Melvin went to his forever home. It helped her, and I'm sure it will help you too."

"I sure hope so because I'm not sure how much longer I can carry around this misery."

Margaret softened her voice. "I lost a baby once too."

"Really? How did you handle it?"

"Not sure I ever did. I still mourn the girl she never grew to be, and that was forty years ago."

"So, the pain never goes away?"

"It never leaves you, but you find ways to live through it. I had a wise old woman tell me once that the Lord weeps with us when we weep because we can't see what He sees. More than once, I heard Him whisper ...*this too shall pass*."

Emma felt at ease with the two women. So much so that for a moment, she thought God placed her on the bus for a reason. She couldn't help but think ...*was a trip to Pinecraft something He had purposely planned for me?*

An unsettling feeling began welling up inside, and she asked, "How long will it take us to arrive in Pinecraft?"

Betty was quick to answer. "You might as well get comfortable. We won't pull into the church parking lot until noon tomorrow."

Emma shook her head. "*Ohhhh* ...Samuel's not going to be pleased."

Margaret's laugh was full of warmth and life. "I can tell you for a fact it won't be the first time, and I'm sure it won't be the last. Both Betty and I were married for well over fifty years when our husbands passed. And I can tell you we both had a few spats we needed to work through."

"*Jah*, but this one's big. Things are already tense at home between us. This is just going to make it worse."

Betty reached across the aisle and twisted to face Emma. "Might be so, but I have to believe God put you in our path for a reason. Trust in Him. Maybe a visit with your *Mommi* Lillian might be part of His bigger plan."

"Betty's right, He's not forgotten you. He might have withheld a child blessing from you to give you a better one."

Emma looked hard at Margaret and asked, "But you lost a baby. How can you suggest losing a child is a blessing?"

Margaret folded her hands, closed her eyes, and laid her head on the back of the seat. "Count my words, child. There *will* be a bigger blessing, I'm sure of it."

Emma stared straight ahead as both women settled in their seats for a nap. A million thoughts were going through her head, but none made much sense. There was no doubt Margaret's statement left her unsettled, and she closed her eyes to push the irritation away. The steady movement of the bus made her eyes heavy, and she found her thoughts being quieted with the faint sound of her *mamm's* voice ringing in her head.

One of the sweetest memories she had of her Amish *mamm*, Stella, was her voice. More than once, she remembered snuggling up on her lap listening to a song. Struggling to remember the tune; she let herself slip into a dream while Stella sang her to sleep.

In the darkest hour, Emma was startled awake by a nightmare. Samuel was calling her name, but she couldn't see him. The anguish in his cry shook her, and it took a few seconds to realize where she was. The hum of the bus tires was the only sound she heard. Both Margaret and Betty were fast asleep, and only the seat behind her had the overhead light switched on. Needing to wash the dream away, she bounced her way to the back of the bus to the restroom. Once inside, diesel fuel fumes overwhelmed her and the blue chemical in the toilet made her hold her breath as she splashed water on her face. The bus followed the curving road, and she found herself jolted in the small room.

Margaret was right. She did have dark rings under her eyes. She washed the sleep from her eyes and straightened her *kapp* in an upright position. Pressing the creases out of her dress she wished she didn't have to wear a mourning dress. Maybe what she needed was to add some color to her life. Just perhaps being away from the prying eyes of her community would help. In Pinecraft, no one but *Mommi*, Betty, and Margaret would know what she was struggling with. Flushing the portable toilet, she quietly opened the door, hoping not to disturb any sleeping passengers.

While making her way back to her seat, she passed a woman reading in the chair behind her. The young woman reached out and tugged on Emma's sleeve. She held her other hand to her lips and moved her knees and invited Emma to sit down.

The young girl couldn't be much older than herself. She wore a soft lavender dress, much like the Mennonite girls from Sugarcreek. Emma slipped in the seat next to her. Then the girl bent her head close to Emma's ear. "I couldn't help but overhear your plight and was hoping I had a chance to talk to you."

Emma didn't say a word but listened intently.

"I lost my baby girl four months ago, and I understand how hard it is to pick yourself back up and go on as if nothing happened. Often, I laid in bed at night and wondered what I could have done differently, but then I'd remember I wasn't alone. Jesus was grieving right beside me."

Emma focused on keeping her breath steady as the woman shared her darkest moments.

"There were days I'd go to the grocery store just so I could walk down the baby aisle. The pain was so real I couldn't seem to escape it, so I understand what you're going through."

Emma folded her hands. "I can't stop thinking about the little things, like his first wiggly tooth or the first scraped knee I should've been able to kiss away."

The young woman dropped her head and murmured, "It was one of the most horrible days of my life. I never even got to bring her home, but I believe God has a plan in my sorrow."

Emma let out a small gasp and asked, "How can you be so confident our pain comes with a purpose?"

The young woman turned to look at Emma. "Because I believe in a God who spared nothing to send His son to die for us. How can I not believe he would take my child for something much bigger and better as well?"

Emma continued, "But when I remember him being cold, I pulled his little blanket tighter even though I knew it wouldn't warm him, my heart breaks in two. How can that be from God?"

"I can't answer that for you, but you can find your answers in the same place I did."

"Where's that?"

The young girl tapped the bible on her lap. "Right here."

Confusion lingered in the air as Emma tried to make sense of the woman's comment. If she could find the answers in there, why hadn't she been taught that? Yes, the ministers in Willow Springs encouraged her to read the bible, but she couldn't understand most of what was written in German. For the first time in months, she felt hopeful. Just being able to open her heart and talk to someone who understood was encouraging.

The girl pulled a tissue from her bag and handed it to Emma. "Don't keep it all bottled up inside. You need to turn to God and believe me, He will help you heal."

Emma tilted her head in the girl's direction and thought, *there it was again ...how could one lone book hold so many answers. Yes, she believed the Lord could do miraculous things, but help her heal and find peace in such hopelessness? Why did everyone keep pointing her to the bible? What was she missing and why hadn't she been able to fight through her loss with God's help thus far?*

The young woman pulled a pencil and piece of paper from her bag and wrote down an address. "My husband is working in Pinecraft for a few weeks, and this is where I'll be staying. If you would like to talk more, you can find me here."

Emma read the girl's name, Lynette Miller, and then tucked it in her pocket. "I don't know how long I'll be staying, so I'm not sure if I'll have time to reach out to you."

The woman wiped her face. "No worries, I wanted to be sure you knew where I'd be if you needed a friend."

Emma slipped out of her seat and mouthed, "Thank you."

CHAPTER 8

Samuel slammed the phone back in its receiver and rested his chin in his hand. It would be days before he could secure a driver to take him to Sugarcreek and another week before catching the bus to Pinecraft. One week before Christmas, and all southbound routes were booked solid. Seven days without a single word from Emma, and his patience was wearing thin.

The drafty phone shanty left him no choice but to make his way back to the house. The unseasonably cold snap blew around his neck as his chest rose and fell with rapid breaths. He stood in the center of the yard, looking in all directions. He could go sulk in the *doddi haus*, return to their new house and get back to work, check on Katie and Daniel, or retreat to the comforts of his *mamm's* kitchen, he chose the latter.

A welcoming smell of coffee and cinnamon circled his head the minute he opened the door. He removed his hat and raked his fingers through his hair before hollering out.

"*Mamm*, just me."

Ruth called from the top of the stairs. "I made fresh cinnamon rolls this morning. Help yourself. I'll be down in a minute."

Samuel kicked off his boots and hung his coat before taking what his mother had offered. Before he had a chance to sit, a burst of cold air entered the room, followed by his father.

"Samuel?"

"*Jah*?"

"What's up?"

Samuel tilted his head quizzically.

"For as long as I've known you, there are two things I can always count on. One, your jaw twitches when your angry, and two, your strides become mammoth when you've got something on your mind."

Samuel poured himself a cup of coffee. "Guess you got me there."

Levi stomped the snow off his boots before slipping out of them. "How about you tell me what's got you so worked up?"

"Might as well wait for *Mamm* so I can explain it to the both of you."

Ruth dropped an armful of laundry by the basement door. "Explain what?"

Levi poured himself a cup of coffee. "What's got Samuel so worked up today."

Ruth stopped at Samuel's side and rested her hand on his shoulder. "Any word from Emma?"

There was a flicker of irritation in Samuel's response. "Not exactly."

Ruth placed a few of the still-warm rolls on a plate and slid them toward Levi. "Where do you think she is?"

"That's what I'm here about. As far as I can gather, she's in Florida."

Ruth brushed crumbs off the counter and dropped them into the sink. "My heavens! When did she decide to do that?"

"I'm not sure. She was supposed to come home two days ago, but as far as I can figure, she set her eyes on a vacation without me."

Ruth pulled a chair away from the table. "Now, son, she hasn't been herself. Perhaps she wasn't ready to come home and face reality yet."

Samuel swallowed hard. "But she never even called to tell me she wasn't coming home!"

Ruth placed her hand over Samuel's clenched fist. "Time is the only thing that fixes this kind of loss. You have to remember her healing is not on your timetable."

Levi stirred a spoon of sugar in his mug. "But Ruth, not telling him where she'd gone, that's unacceptable."

Ruth's voice tempered. "In whose view?"

Levi brought his cup to his lips, looked over its rim, and then nodded in Samuel's direction. "In his, of course."

Ruth placed a gooey roll on the napkin in front of her. "Have either of you carried a baby under your heart only to have it snatched from you at a moment's notice?"

Silence filled the air as both men swayed their heads from side to side.

"Husband, what you fail to remember is the despair I went through when we lost not one child, but three. How can you forget the months of agony I went through just to get out of bed in the morning?'

Levi lowered his head. "I suppose so. But to run off to Florida without letting your husband know where you've gone. I can't imagine you ever acting so irresponsible."

"No, because I still had Samuel to take care of. What does Emma have to come back to but an empty home?"

Samuel pushed the sticky dessert away. "She has me, our life, and a brand-new house."

"Samuel, I understand how upset you are that she didn't clear it with you first, but as a woman, I sympathize with what's going on inside of her. Here, she has to pretend everything is okay because that's what she's been trained to do, but inside, her heart is torn in two."

Ruth took a bite and waited a few moments before continuing. "Until she finds her way, she's like a wind in a passing storm. This is a season for her, and she has to fight her way back in her own way, in her own time."

"But I wanted us to have a fresh start by moving into the new house before Christmas, and she's gone and upset all my plans."

Ruth's voice took on a new octave. "The major difference between men and women. Men become workaholics, and most times, avoid the issue. Women, on the other hand, mourn the things they can't hold onto ...smells, touches, a baby in their arms."

Ruth took a sip of coffee. "Give her time, but most of all, go after her. Don't let her think she has to do it alone."

Samuel stared into his cup. "I'm to blame."

Levi leaned back in his chair. "There was nothing you could have done any differently to prevent God from calling your son home."

Samuel tapped his fingers on the table. "Perhaps so, but I still feel like I failed my family."

Ruth wiped her mouth with a napkin. "You haven't failed, and you can prove it by finding a way to bring her home. A woman needs her husband to go out of his way for her. Chase her down and show you won't let her battle alone."

***

Emma opened her eyes when Margaret tapped her shoulder. "We're here, sleepyhead, wake up."

The eager voice of her new friend made it impossible to be anything but excited about arriving in Pinecraft. For twenty-two hours, she ran through an array of emotions about her quick decision to veer off course. There was no turning back now. All she could do was embrace her hasty diversion.

The sun burned through her dark stockings and black coverings the minute she stepped off the bus. A bustle of passengers zealous in greeting their friends added to her excitement; clear down to the soles of her black boots.

A display of brightly colored apparel and flip-flops swarmed with smiling faces. There was no doubt the people who came to this small town found joy in their surroundings. Everything around her seemed fresh and inviting, and for a minute, she accepted a new viewpoint on life.

Margaret and Betty stood in front of her, receiving multiple hugs and well wishes from long-time friends. She learned during their late-night conversations that both had been coming to Sarasota every winter for the past ten years. They called it their home ...one step closer to heaven. Emma didn't understand it at the time, but the sunshine and the lingering sweet smell of blooming flowers mingled together with the sea breeze made her grasp the meaning.

She reached out and pulled on Betty's sleeve. "You're right; this place is one step closer to heaven."

Betty warmly smiled and looped her arm through hers. "And the best of what this town has to offer is just a short bus ride away."

Emma tipped her chin toward the older woman. "How can it be any better than this?"

"The ocean, silly girl." Betty pointed to a street sign. "Follow Bahia Vista Street west for two and a half miles, and you'll find yourself in Sarasota Bay. Better yet, catch a city bus, and in less than thirty minutes, you can be to Siesta Key on the Gulf Coast."

Margaret reached down to pick up her bag. "My advice is if you want to see heaven on earth, spend some time digging your toes in the white sand and going for a swim in the Bay."

All thoughts of home fluttered away as Margaret described the pearl white sand and crystal-clear water of the Gulf Coast. For the first time in two months, Emma felt she could restore a little of her life by immersing herself in the beauty of winter in Florida.

From across the parking lot, she heard her name.

"Emma, Emma Yoder."

There was no mistaking the soft voice of *Mommi* Lillian.

Emma broke free of Betty's grip and ran to her grandmother. "How did you know I was coming?"

Lillian held her arms open. "I knew no such thing. I walked up to meet the bus hoping I'd see some friends, and low and behold, you stepped off the bus."

Emma rested her chin on *Mommi* Lillian's shoulder for a long minute and enjoyed the warm embrace. Lillian pushed her away and looked at her with a loving smile. "What a wonderful surprise." She looked over her shoulder. "Where's Samuel? Is he fetching your bags?"

With a twinge of regret she replied, "He didn't come."

Lillian looped her arm through hers and patted her hand, "Maybe a few days away from the cold is just what you need to erase those worry lines from your eyes."

Emma lifted her head and took a deep breath through her nose. "What is that I smell?"

"Winter Jasmine. Isn't it heavenly?"

Emma glanced down at her grandmother. "You have no idea how badly I needed this. I hope you don't mind I came unannounced?"

"Heavens no. My *schwester* Martha and I enjoy the company. Come, pick up your bag and we'll get you settled."

Emma walked back toward the bus and stood beside Lynette, waiting for their bags to be unloaded from the storage compartment.

Lynette leaned in closer. "I'm serious. If you need a friend while you're here, please don't hesitate to call on me. My husband is a minister and is preaching here for the next few weeks. We'd love it if you would join us on Sunday."

Emma looked over the bus toward the stucco building. "A minister? But you're so young."

Lynette smiled and answered, "When the Lot falls upon you; God doesn't take age into account."

"I suppose not."

Lynette nodded her head in the direction of the street behind the bus. "There's Alvin now. Please, reach out to me, but more importantly, join us on Sunday."

Emma watched as Lynette picked up her suitcase and waved at her husband. It was hard for Emma to pull herself away from watching the friendly way Alvin greeted her. How was it her new friend, who had just lost a baby herself, greeted her husband with so much tenderness? With a rush of remorse, she knew she had to find a phone ...and quickly.

Once she found her way back to her grandmother, Lillian was talking with Margaret and Betty. "I hear my quilting friends kept you company and convinced you to come."

"They sure did, and if it wasn't for them, I'd still be in the cold instead of wanting to shed some of these layers before I have a heat-stroke."

"Oh goodness, let's go home so you can change into something lighter."

"That might be a problem since all I have is my heavy winter clothing with me."

Margaret spoke up. "No problem, follow us. My granddaughter is about your size, and she leaves her Florida clothes here. They will be perfect for you to borrow."

"Are you sure?"

"You bet. Besides, she's stuck in Ohio. Baby number three is on the way, and her husband feels they should stay put this winter."

Emma, Lillian, and Betty followed Margaret down the center of Graber Street, chatting about who had arrived at the bus and how long everyone was staying. It was as if the whole community revolved around the bus schedule. The church parking lot cleared out as smiling families made their way to their winter homes throughout the small community.

Lillian turned toward Emma. "What is the long face about all of a sudden?"

Emma whispered, "I need to find a phone to call Samuel."

"As soon as we get to Martha's. She has one of those flip phones in the house for emergencies."

The thought of calling Samuel left her a bit uneasy. They'd left things in such a state before she went to Marie's. This was only going to add to his frustration. Suddenly, a thought came to her. *Maybe she could convince him to come to Florida.* *"Mommi,* do you think Martha would be okay if Samuel met me here?"

"I think that's a wonderful idea, and I'm sure she would be fine with it. We can ask her as soon as we get home."

Margaret pointed to the house on the corner of Fry and Graber Street. "Here we are. Come in, ladies, while I find a few dresses for Emma."

She unlocked the door, and a cool breeze met them as they followed her inside. The Florida heat forced them to allow the comforts of electric air conditioning even if an oil lamp was positioned in the middle of the kitchen table. Most who visited the area still held tight to their rules and practices, while others enjoyed the temporary reprieve from the strict ordained regulations of their home community. Margaret and Betty were two who opted to follow their New Order ways as much as possible, all while enjoying the sun and warm temperatures of wintering in the south.

Margaret set her suitcase down and disappeared into a small room at the back of the house. When she returned, she carried three light-colored dresses along with a pair of flip-flops dangling from her finger.

"Here you go. These should work for you while you're here."

Emma looked at the pink, yellow, and purple short sleeve dresses. Her features took on a distressed look. "*Denki*, but I'm not sure I should wear things so colorful."

Betty opened a drawer by the back door and took out a yellow plastic grocery bag and held it open so Margaret could slip the stack of dresses inside. "Emma, these colors may not be acceptable at home, but you're in Pinecraft now. And here they are perfectly fine."

"But I'm still in my mourning period."

Lillian wrapped her arm around Emma's shoulders. "The dark circles under your eyes tell the world more than you think. It's completely your choice, but it wouldn't hurt if you traded your heavy winter clothing for something lighter for the short time you'll be here."

Emma took the bag and flip-flops. "I'll think about it."

Lillian squeezed her shoulder into her own. "You do that. In the meantime, let's go home so you can rest some before supper. I'm excited to introduce you to my *schwester*."

***

After introductions, Emma borrowed Martha's cell phone. She escaped to the little porch at the front of *Mommi* Lillian's *schwester's* house. After dialing the number to the phone shanty at the end of the lane at home, she waited, hoping someone would answer. They had the answering machine set to pick up on the fifteenth ring, giving anyone outside plenty of time to respond before she'd have to leave a message.

She held her breath the entire time and only relaxed enough to fill her lungs when she heard it click over so she could record a message. A million thoughts raced through her head before she listened to the beep, and then the line went dead. Confused, she dialed again and waited for fifteen rings for the same thing to happen. She flipped the phone closed and leaned back in the white wicker rocker.

The mid-afternoon sun was high in the sky, and the heat radiating from the rays fluttered across her face as she tilted toward the warmth. She still hadn't decided if she should change into the dress Margaret had loaned her. But after a few minutes, sweat rolled down her back and in the creases of her elbows under the polyester fabric of her long black mourning dress. She scurried off to the bedroom at the back of the house. After laying out all three dresses on the bed, she chose the pale yellow one, took off the heavy dress, and slipped the summery lightweight fabric over her head. She removed her long black stockings and enjoyed the cool tile on her toes before slipping her feet into the simple black sandals. She didn't even pick the pile of clothes off the floor before she tiptoed through the living room trying not to disturb the now napping *schwester's*.

A family on tricycles passed by and waved in her direction as she stepped off the porch. Taking note of Martha's house number, she took off. Free ...if only momentarily from the cold surrounding her soul, she walked down Gilbert Avenue. She wasn't sure what she hoped to find, but for a little while, Emma hoped to shed her anguish much like the crumbled clothes she left behind in exchange for something brighter and more untroublesome.

CHAPTER 9

Heat rose from the pavement, but Emma hardly noticed as she weaved her way through the side streets in and around Martha's house. The small cottages, painted in soft tropical colors, were lined with white picket fences and palm trees. Each yard was as neat as a pin and had a plentiful supply of colorful flowers that added to the landscape. A group of young girls toting a volleyball and picnic basket turned in front of her. Their giggles and chatter made her miss Katie and her twin *schwesters*, Rebecca and Anna. There was a time before her *mamm* died, and long before she found out she was born to an *Englisher,* that the carefree days of her youth were plentiful.

The group of girls kicked their shoes off and dug their feet in the sand at the volleyball court at Pinecraft Park. It only took a few minutes; before each side was packed, a mixture of girls and boys. She leaned on the fence separating the court from the street for only a minute before walking past two older gentlemen playing shuffleboard. Everyone was engrossed in something at the open-air picnic shelter, be it a game of checkers or a mid-afternoon snack.

A playground across the parking lot enticed her to find a seat on a single swing. She kicked off her flip-flops and let white sand spill over her toes. Closing her eyes, she pushed the swing into motion and let the breeze cover her face as she pumped her legs harder and harder. Without realizing it, she felt joy, something she hadn't allowed herself to partake in for a very long time. Jumping off the swing, as she did as a child, she flew through the air and then waited until the seat came to a complete stop before turning away and walking back to a picnic table.

From somewhere behind her, a sweet voice made its way closer. "Now, if I were forty years younger, I might give that a try myself."

Emma turned toward the woman. "*Jah*, I can't believe I did that. It's been a while since I've done anything so childish. I'm surprised I didn't hurt myself." Emma rubbed the spot on her lower stomach, half regretting her impulsive decision.

The petite woman sat down beside her. "Mary, Mary Miller. And you?"

"Emma Yoder."

"I haven't seen you around. Did you just arrive on the bus from Sugarcreek today?"

"I did. How did you know?"

The woman let out a slight snicker before answering. "Not much gets by me around here. You could say I'm the unofficial tour guide of Pinecraft."

The two women sat and watched a group of small children chase a skink under a nearby picnic table. The lizard ran from the squeals and right over Emma's foot. She shrieked, and the small towhead boy stopped in front of her. His big brown eyes looked tenderly at her when he said, "Skinks, don't bite."

Emma patted the little boy on the top of his head, "Thanks for explaining it to me."

His black pants, tiny suspenders, and baby blue shirt ran off; blending into the group of children heading to the playground.

Mary pointed to a family gathered under a big oak tree covered in Spanish moss. "He's the youngest of that family.

They have eight *kinner*. Seems like every time they come, they have another one in tow."

Finding it hard to take her eyes away from the young family, she asked, "How long have you been coming?"

"Some twenty years now, but I don't visit; I live here full-time over on Gilbert Avenue. My husband was a minister here before he passed. I love it here so much I couldn't imagine going back to Ohio, so I stayed."

"Miller? Gilbert Avenue? I met a girl on the bus, Lynette Miller."

"Daughter-in-law." Mary shook her head and made a ...tsk-tsk sound with her tongue. "So sad ...she and my son lost their first child a short time ago. My son, Alvin, came down a few weeks ago, but Lynette had to stay behind for a couple of doctor's appointments before they cleared her for travel."

Emma crossed her legs and leaned her arms on the picnic table behind her. "We have a lot in common."

"Who? You and Lynette?"

"*Jah.*"

Emma didn't allude to her meaning but instead stood to leave. "It was nice to meet you, Mary."

"And you as well." Mary stood and said, "289."

"Two eighty-nine?"

"Our address, 289 Gilbert Avenue. You're always welcome, and if you want a tour of Pinecraft, stop and see me. I'm sure Lynette would love to visit with you."

Mary Miller had a way about her that told Emma it wouldn't be the last time she'd be seeing Pinecraft's resident tour guide.

***

Samuel stood at the calendar and stared aimlessly at it. How could the love of his life go ten days without finding any way to reach him? He checked the phone almost hourly and practically waited at the end of the lane each day for the mailman. If she did go to Pinecraft, she would have arrived two days ago, plenty of time to call and leave a message for him. With each passing day, the hollow spot to the right of his heart ached a little deeper.

A steady knock broke his stance, and he moved to the front room. As he pulled the door open, Bishop Weaver stood with his hand in the air, ready to announce his arrival again.

"Samuel, may I have a word with you?"

Samuel opened the door wider and let the bishop cross the threshold. After closing the door, he pointed to the two rockers near the front window.

The bishop removed his black felt hat and balanced it on his knee. "I didn't see you or Emma in church yesterday."

"No, sir, you didn't."

Samuel didn't offer an explanation even though Bishop Weaver allowed plenty of time before he posed another statement. "The both of you need the support of your church family as much as you need each other."

Samuel clenched the arms of his chair as he let the bishop continue.

"Been my experience that tragedy like this often triggers some big questions."

Bishop Weaver set the chair in motion as he waited for Samuel to respond. When he didn't, he asked, "Has that happened?"

Samuel followed the bishop's movement and answered, "Could be." He didn't feel it was his place to confess Emma's anger at God or her statement that they must have done something wrong to anger Him. So instead, he let his answer stand.

The bishop looked toward the kitchen. "Is Emma here? I'd like to speak to her."

"She's not. She went to Sugarcreek."

Bishop Weaver crumpled his bushy eyebrows and rested his foot flat on the floor to stop the chair from rocking. "Alone?"

"*Jah.*"

Clearing his throat and setting his tone a bit softer he said, "The death of a child can bring a couple closer, or it can isolate them from one another. However, what you need to understand is every marriage will be strained after a loss like this. It's normal, and I don't want either of you to feel ashamed if that happens."

Bishop Weaver had been the head of his church for as long as he could remember, and not once in his twenty-three years had he witnessed this side of him.

Samuel tilted his chin in his direction, unsure how to respond.

The bishop stood and headed to the door. "Samuel, I'm not as coldhearted as you may think, and you aren't the first couple I've seen stumble after the loss of a child."

Samuel stood and turned to look out the window. The older man walked to his side. For a few minutes, they stayed silent, watching the birds outside the window.

Before turning back toward the door, Bishop Weaver changed his tone to something more recognizable. "Marriages only work when two people are together."

Samuel waited until the weathered man stepped outside and shut the door before he mumbled. "One has to have a wife who wants to be home to make things work."

The clock on the kitchen wall chimed ten times just as the hired driver pulled up to the front porch. In three hours, he'd be on a bus to Florida and one day closer to bringing his wife home where she belonged.

***

Lillian and Emma sat at a table on the shaded side of the Coffee Café. Emma stood in line for over twenty minutes, waiting to let her grandmother buy a couple of their signature drinks. According to her *Mommi*, the Iced Honey Lavender Latté was to die for. While waiting, she took notice that everyone she met greeted her with a smile. There definitely was something in the air in Pinecraft, and she hoped she could carry whatever it was back to Willow Springs. After ordering, she headed back to the table to wait for her number to be called. Mary Miller and her daughter-in-law, Lynette, walked up, and Mary pointed to the two empty chairs. "Do you mind if we share your table?"

Emma pulled the chair out closest to her. "Please do."

Lynette brushed a stray hair behind her ear and wiped her hand across her forehead. "It always takes me a few days to get acclimated to the temperature when I first arrive."

Emma snickered before commenting. "*Mommi* had a sweater on this morning, and it was all I could do to keep from sweating."

Mary took a sip of her frosted drink. "Give it a few days, and you'll find the air conditioners are a bit too cold for you as well."

Lynette hung her purse over the chair and moved so she was sitting in the shade. "I hoped Alvin and I could go to the beach this afternoon, but he wanted to work on his sermon for Sunday. He promised we could sneak away tomorrow."

"Order 289."

Emma looked to the pick-up window. "I'll be right back."

Lillian took the opportunity to lean into Lynette to whisper, "Do you think Emma could go to the beach with you?"

Lynette smiled, assuring Lillian it was a great idea.

Emma sipped her drink as she walked back to the table. "*Mommi*, this is wonderful. Thanks for suggesting it."

Lillian took a long drink before she looked warmly at Emma. "Lynette and her husband are going to Siesta Key tomorrow. I think it would be a great way for you to enjoy all that Sarasota has to offer."

Emma pushed her straw around in her drink. "The beach? I've never seen the ocean before, but I'm not sure."

Mary added, "As your official tour guide, I would highly suggest you get out of your comfort zone and take the city bus to the Keys with Alvin and Lynette. You won't be sorry. Something about that white sugar sand chases all worry right out into the ocean."

Emma stayed quiet as Lillian, Mary and Lynette went on talking about the beach. Something didn't feel quite right. Samuel weighed heavy on her mind. She should be sharing this experience with her husband ...not alone. There were too many unsettled things between her and Samuel to relax enough to enjoy her visit. If she could at least talk to Samuel and explain to him why she didn't come home, maybe she could feel better about going off and taking pleasure in a day at the beach. All she could do was keep trying to call him.

Mary placed her phone on the table next to her pocketbook. "Mary, would you mind if I used your phone to try to call my husband?

"No, of course, help yourself."

Emma picked up the phone and excused herself from the table. The ice cream shop across the street wasn't open for business yet, so all the picnic tables out front sat empty. Taking it as an opportunity to escape the busy Coffee Café, she crossed the street to one of the ice cream shop's red umbrellas. Turning her back to the busy street noise, she prayed someone would answer Levi and Ruth's phone. Just like the five or more times she tried over the last few days, the phone rang and rang but didn't allow her to leave a message before disconnecting. She dialed her father's furniture shop in a last-ditch effort to get news to someone in Willow Springs.

On the third ring, a familiar voice answered.

"Byler's Furniture."

"*Datt.*"

Without even so much as a hello, her father began to scold her. "Where are you? You have Samuel and everyone else in this family worried sick about you. We know you've been troubled, but I raised you better than this. This is unacceptable behavior."

"*Datt*, let me explain."

"You owe me no explanation, but you do owe one to Samuel."

"Listen, you have every right to be upset with me, and yes, I need to talk to Samuel, and I've been trying. The phone at Levi's won't let me leave a message. I've tried several times, but before I can leave a message, it hangs up."

"I'll tell Levi to check the answering machine. But again, it shouldn't have even been an issue. You should have come home when you said you would."

"Can you deliver a message to Samuel?"

"*Nee*. He left this morning for Sugarcreek."

"What is he going there for?"

"Why wouldn't he go there? He went to bring you home."

"*Datt*...I'm not in Sugarcreek."

"Daughter, where are you?"

"Florida."

The sigh on the other end of the phone matched the squeak of her father's office chair as he plopped down. Even with being over a thousand miles apart, she could envision the slump of her father's shoulders.

Jacob cleared his throat. "You could have at least let Marie and Nathan know what you had planned."

"I didn't plan any of it. It just happened, and I didn't give it much thought before I stepped on a bus going to Sarasota."

"I half suspect you aren't giving much of anything a thought these days but yourself."

"*Datt,* that's pretty harsh considering all I've been through."

"There comes a time when you need to surrender your life to the Lord's will and quit fighting it."

A stillness laid between them as Emma tried to gauge her words, trying to keep her voice from cracking.

"Even when ...you think ...God is punishing you?"

"Why would you think that?"

"Why else would he take James from us? Samuel or I must have done something to displease Him."

"Emma, God doesn't work like that."

"Then please, *Datt*, explain it to me."

"What's to explain? Our job is to work hard to follow our ways, just like our ancestors have done for hundreds of years. You're not the only woman who has lost a child. How do you think all the women before you handled it?"

"That's just it. I have no idea and that's what I'm struggling with."

"I'll tell you how. They moved on and accepted it as God's will for their life."

Taking a few moments to calm her racing pulse she added, "I can't accept it's all that easy."

"We all have questions on how God works, but it's not our place to question, but to obey. Plus, when our time is up and we face our maker, then we'll truly know whether we've worked hard enough to get our questions answered."

A heaviness pressed on Emma's shoulders. "Oh ...*Datt*, I have so many questions."

"And rightly so, but you need to take those questions to the Lord. Or perhaps you need to get yourself home and meet with Bishop Weaver."

"You're right, but first, I need to track down Samuel. I'll call Nathan's office. Hopefully, Nathan can give Samuel a message from me. I'm sure he'll head to Marie's first."

Her father took in a deep breath and exhaled loudly before replying, "Good."

Emma took in a small breath before asking, "Do you know anything about the letter *Mamm* left with Ruth for me?"

"No, why?"

"Before I left to go to Marie's, Ruth gave me a box with a shawl *Mamm* had crocheted for me, along with a letter instructing me to find the truth in Jesus."

With a deep groan, Jacob answered, "Ohhhh...I prayed she kept that to herself."

"Why would you want her to do that?"

"Have you showed that letter to anyone else?"

"Only Katie. Why are you so upset?"

"Emma, you need to forget that letter ever existed and rely on what you've been taught. Any other notion will only cause turmoil in the community, and I'd hate for you to be the source of that."

"You're scaring me. Why would this upset you so?"

"Please just trust your *Datt*. I know what's best concerning this matter."

Emma's heartbeat quickened. There was something in her father's tone that was alarming. "*Datt*, I need to go; I want to try to reach Samuel."

After saying their goodbyes, Emma closed the phone and played her father's warning over in her head. There had been only one other time in her life when her father's voice took on a hopeless tone, and that was when he told her she wasn't his biological daughter. Now for some reason, his plea took on a whole new level of uneasiness.

Still, deep in thought, she started to cross the street back to the Café when she practically stepped out in front of a passing car. A horn diverted her attention back to the present, and she jumped back on the sidewalk. Her eyes, still fixated on the back of the car, read its license plate. EPH 0289.

CHAPTER 10

S omewhere outside of Columbia, SC, the bus Samuel was on broke down, leaving him stranded. For ten hours, he sat inside a bus terminal, waiting for another to continue his journey to Sarasota.

Three days before Christmas, and he was no closer to getting Emma back home where she belonged than he was twelve days ago. The clock on the wall above the bus departure digital board clicked away. With every passing minute, Samuel's jaw twitched and clenched so hard he gave himself a headache. In the background, Christmas music played, and happy travelers anxiously waited for their connection.

He walked to the electronic board, looking for bus number 289. The ticket agent informed him the board would announce when the new bus arrived. As if on cue, bus 289 blinked on the screen as a woman's voice played over the speaker. "Passengers awaiting Bus 289 to Sarasota can make their way to Loading Zone E."

Swinging the small duffle bag over his shoulder, he mumbled, "About time." Falling in line behind a group of blue and black-clad elderly, he let a woman with small children step in line before him. An array of white prayer *kapps* in all different sizes made their way up the stairs. The stress the delay caused was evident on the mother's face as she tried to calm the littlest one. With one hand on the littlest girl and one around a baby she held tight in her arms, she whispered something in the girl's ear, which in turn made her cry. The woman looked up at Samuel and pleaded. "Sir, would you mind holding my son for a minute? My daughter is dead set against getting on the bus, I need to pick her up."

The woman's eyes pleaded, and he obliged. She placed the sleeping infant in his arms in one swift swoop, and he waited until she led all three of her daughters on the bus. Shuffling the baby to his other arm, he handed the bus driver his ticket and looked to where the driver pointed. "You are in row E, seat 2."

Samuel kicked his bag under his seat, laid the child across his lap, and pulled his arms out of his heavy jacket. South

Carolina was already warmer than Ohio, and he wished he would have worn a lighter jacket. The small blue bundle started to squirm, and he instantly brought him to his chest. He followed the sound of a crying child and tried to get the young mother's attention. When she caught his eye, she mouthed, "Thank you."

When the last of the passengers boarded, the driver apologized for the inconvenience and promised they would arrive in Pinecraft by nine that evening. Samuel laid his head against the back of the seat and closed his eyes. Nine o'clock? How would he ever find Emma, let alone lodging for the night? His day was getting worse by the minute.

An hour passed, but Samuel still held the sleeping infant in his lap. When the child started to stir, he glanced over his shoulder to see his mother fast asleep, resting the petite girl over her shoulder. Not sure what he would do if the child was hungry. He gently removed a layer of the blanket and whispered, "Bear with me. It looks like your *mamm* needs a rest. Perhaps you'd like some of these layers off." Not one second after he removed the blanket, the boy shot his hands above his head. The child stretched, arching his back and cooing simultaneously. Samuel smiled before whispering, "I bet that feels good. I wouldn't like to be wound up like a mummy either." Samuel shook the last of the blanket from the boy's feet and propped him over his shoulder. It took only a few minutes for the boy to fall back asleep, and Samuel tried to do the same.

The baby's fine hair rubbed up against Samuel's cheek, and he couldn't help but lean into the softness. He'd never held a baby before, but for some reason, it felt natural. The child, not much more than a few months old, warmed a spot in his heart. He rested his head on the back of the chair and let the hum of the bus tires sway him deep in thought. *We'll have more kinner, I'm sure of it. We're just going through one of those tough spots the bishop spoke of. Things will be better once I get Emma home.*

A light tap to his shoulder brought him out of his head and back to the young woman leaning over him.

"I can't thank you enough; Maryann finally fell asleep, and God willing, the girls will stay settled until we arrive in Pinecraft."

Samuel handed her the blue blanket and shifted the child to his mother's arms.

"It was no trouble, but I was surprised you asked. There are plenty of women on the bus who would have made a better babysitter for sure."

The woman tucked the blanket under her arm. "But none who could rescue me in a moment's notice."

Stretching his legs out in front of him, he asked, "What's his name?"

"James Paul."

The woman turned and headed back to her seat without noticing the deep raspy moan he tried to conceal. It was as if October 15th happened all over again the minute she whispered his name. For the last ten weeks he kept busy, fearing reality would crash down on him if he sat still too long. Holding the woman's child brought all those memories flooding back so fast he had to blow out a couple of long breaths to calm his racing pulse.

***

Promptly at nine o'clock, the bus pulled into Pinecraft, Florida and the overhead lights flashed on. Samuel looked out the window to find a group of people gathered under a nearby streetlight. He assumed most passengers found a way to tell waiting family when their bus would arrive. When he stepped out into the parking lot, he fought to focus past the lights for anything that resembled a hotel. No one knew he was coming, so there wouldn't be anyone to greet him. The parking lot was empty, and the bus pulled away. Leaving him alone in a strange town with no idea how to find Emma. Noise across the street drew his attention, and he wandered toward the sound. Walking through a seating area of the darkened Coffee Café, he found himself in front of the Dairy Bar. Ice cream would have to do in place of a regular meal until he could find his way around.

A group of young men was sitting at the table next to him. "Excuse me, would any of you happen to know Lillian Shetler?"

One of the sandy-haired boys answered, "I don't know that name, but there were quite a few new faces playing volleyball this afternoon. Could she have been one of them?"

Samuel took a bite of his chocolate sundae. "Lillian is my wife's grandmother, so I'm pretty sure she wouldn't have been playing volleyball."

Two boys, in unison, said, "I guess not."

The first boy piped in. "We just arrived last week, so we haven't met too many people yet."

Samuel dropped his head. "Thanks anyway."

Another one of the boys stated, "My parents talked to some lady over on Gilbert Avenue when we first got here. Folks say she is Pinecraft's unofficial tour guide. You might want to pay her a visit. I think her name was Mary or Mildred ...something like that."

Samuel perked up. "You wouldn't happen to know the exact address, would you?"

"Nope. All I know for sure is it was Gilbert Avenue."

"Thanks anyway. Could you point me in the direction of something to eat besides ice cream?"

One of the boys pointed down the street. "Dutch Family Restaurant is right down the road. But they're closed now. Opens back up in the morning at seven."

Samuel took the last bite of his ice cream and threw the dish away and tipped his hat in their direction. "Thanks, boys."

It was too late to go knocking on doors, so he headed back to the church parking lot, used his duffle bag for a pillow, and laid down in the alcove of the church's entrance.

***

The heat from the sand penetrated Emma's thin flip-flops as she struggled to walk through the foreign matter. She carried her heavy beach bag, loaded down with everything her grandmother thought she might need for a day at the beach.

Lynette fell into step with Emma. "We have our favorite spot over by the volleyball court, it's not much further, and hopefully, there will be a free picnic table we can snatch up."

Emma switched her bag to the other arm. "Thank you so much for letting me tag along. It was fun riding the bus over here and having you point out all the landmarks along the way. You're giving me a true feel of Sarasota. I'm starting to realize why everyone loves it here so much."

Alvin piped in, "It has its good points, but I wouldn't trade Sugarcreek for it permanently. I like the snow."

Lynette elbowed Emma and whispered loud enough her husband heard. "Don't let him fool you. He only likes the snow because of hunting."

"My husband Samuel likes to hunt too."

Without missing a beat, Alvin asked, "Why didn't your husband come with you?"

"Alvin, I don't think that's any of our business," Lynette stated.

Emma tried to lighten her response, all while knowing it was more of an issue than she wanted to make it. "Long story, but I came to Pinecraft on the spur of the moment."

Alvin didn't respond and kept moving forward. After they made it to the picnic table under the shade of the oak tree near the volleyball net, Lynette dropped her bag and made a rush to the water. "I've been waiting for this moment all year. I'm wasting no time dipping my toes in the ocean."

Alvin waved his wife on. "Go, enjoy yourself. I'll get things set up here and join you in a minute."

Emma took a blue and white tablecloth from her bag and flipped it over the table before setting a small cooler on the corner to keep it in place.

Alvin arranged their beach supplies in a neat pile and sat facing the ocean, watching his wife splash her feet in the salty water. "Good to see her smile."

Emma sat next to him and took in the picture-perfect view. "It's lovely. How can you not come here and smile?"

For a long while they both sat on the bench, watching Lynette enjoy herself.

Alvin leaned his arms back on the table and stretched his feet out in front of him, crossing them at his ankles. Moments passed before Alvin continued, "Lynette said you lost a baby recently too."

Emma's stomach lurched. "*Jah.*"

Something was comforting knowing her new friends understood what she was going through. So much so that she didn't think twice about openly talking about it.

"I still can't believe it. I struggle with thinking there had to be something I could have done differently or some other way to prevent it."

Alvin leaned over and rested his elbows on his knees. "Lynette had the same questions." He waited to gather his thoughts. "I'm always reminded that Jesus pleaded with God for another option just before his death. But in the end, he knew there was no other way."

Emma bounced her foot while contemplating a response. "Everyone keeps telling us there's a reason God put us on this path, but I don't understand what good could come out of taking our child."

Alvin moved his head in her direction. "Most likely, He wants you to draw closer to Him."

"Perhaps, but I'm not feeling very close to God these days."

"Have you tried reaching out to Him? Communication is more than a one-way street."

"Not too much. I just don't feel like God talks to me. I'm not sure how I feel, but right now, there's not much love left in my heart."

Alvin twisted her way. "I'd say the good Lord sent you to Pinecraft, so He could work on that heart of yours."

Emma stood. "Maybe so, but right now, that ocean is looking pretty inviting."

***

As soon as the first ray of sunshine made its way above the horizon, Samuel ate a quick bite at the restaurant the boys had told him about. Afterward, he walked the streets that weaved behind the church. Stopping an older gentleman, Samuel asked how to find Gilbert Avenue. If he had to, he'd knock on every door until he found the tour guide the boys mentioned. Surely this woman would know where he could find Emma's grandmother. Standing at the crossroads of Gilbert Avenue and Fry Street, he looked up and down both ends, hoping something would guide his way.

"Looks like you could use some direction."

Samuel turned toward the petite woman on an adult size tricycle. "I sure could. I'm looking for a woman on Gilbert Avenue with the name of Mary or Mildred."

"My name is Mary, and I live on Gilbert Avenue."

"You wouldn't happen to be the woman they call the tour guide of Pinecraft?"

Mary smiled before responding. "Are you looking for a tour?"

Samuel breathed a sigh of relief. "I'm hoping you might point me to where Lillian Shetler might be staying."

"Family?"

"She's my wife's grandmother."

"Emma?"

"Yes, Emma, have you seen her?"

Mary placed her hand over her chest. "Oh, thank the Lord."

Samuel shifted his duffle bag to the other shoulder. "So, my Emma's here, for certain?"

"*Jah.* She just left to go to Siesta Key to spend the day at the beach."

"The beach? Can you tell me how to get there?"

Mary took a folded map from her bike basket and outlined the path to the closest bus stop. "It will take you about an hour, but I think they're planning on staying all day."

"They? She didn't go alone?"

"Heaven's no. The beach is more fun with friends."

Samuel positioned the map to line up with the direction he needed to go and thanked Mary for her help.

He headed off, but not before Mary stopped him. "Give me your bag and coat and let me drop it off at Lillian's. It's too hot for you to be lugging it to the beach."

After securing his belongings in her basket, he thanked her again and took off in a steady jog toward the bus stop.

***

Palm tree-lined sidewalks and sandy pathways met Samuel as he maneuvered through people making their way to the beach. It was ten o'clock, and the parking lot at the entrance to Siesta Beach was filling up. His eyes darted past the sparsely dressed women. Never had he seen such a display and found himself dropping his chin in hopes of blocking most of it out. When a young group of brightly dressed Amish girls came into view, he hoped Emma might be close by. His heavy work boots dug deep impressions in the sand, and his winter hat felt much out of place. Sweat was running between his shoulder blades, and he stopped for a moment to look up and down the miles of beach that stared back at him.

Choosing to move toward the group of girls, he stopped when Emma's frame came into view. There was no doubt it was her, even though she was dressed in light purple and not her required black mourning dress. Adrenaline mixed with a comforting warmth filled him from head to toe as he walked her way. He had no intention of eavesdropping, but there was something in the way the man's friendliness bothered him. What on earth was she thinking sitting so close to another man in public. His jaw clenched, and he balled his hands tightly.

Emma's words ... *there's not much love left in my heart* ...cut a hole in his stomach, and he swallowed hard. There was nothing he could say, so he turned and walked away.

The path back to the bus stop seemed like an eternity. He played the conversation over in his head. *Why on earth would she share something so personal ...something she needed to share with him first ...something only he should hear? Of course, she didn't feel close to him. She up and left without so much of a word. How could she be seen in public sitting so close to another man?*

The scene blinded his vision so much that his temples throbbed, and he had to blink hard to find his seat back on a bus heading back to Pinecraft.

CHAPTER 11

Samuel tightly wrapped his fingers around the glass of tea Lillian handed him. "I'm sure they'll be back anytime now. Emma will be so happy you're here. She fretted when she couldn't reach you on the phone."

"She tried to call?"

"Of course. At least five or six times. For some reason, it wouldn't let her leave a message. I'm pretty sure she called her father a day or two ago."

Samuel's stomach rolled, but he didn't tell Lillian he saw Emma and her friends at the beach. For all she knew, he couldn't find them and headed back to Pinecraft.

Lillian took a seat on the front porch beside him and used a small paper fan to stir the air. "Do you think you'll be able to stay until after Christmas? It sure would be nice to have family with us this holiday."

He took a long drink and gave Lillian a halfhearted smile. The last thing he wanted to think of was staying any longer than he had to. First and foremost, he needed to have a few words with his wife, and then he would be on his way back to Pennsylvania. With or without her.

Laughter bounced off the small cottages, and he heard Emma's voice long before she came into view. He stiffened his shoulders as she made the way up the sidewalk. Sun kissed her cheekbones, and her shorter than usual dress swayed in the breeze. Her face widened when she caught his eye, and she dropped the beach bag and ran to him. "Samuel, you found me."

He walked to the edge of the step and crossed his arms over his chest. In a harsh tone. "*Jah.*"

Her smile faded, and she turned toward Alvin and Lynette, who waited at the foot of the stairs. "Samuel, these are my new friends, Alvin and Lynette. They're from Sugarcreek and are visiting Pinecraft for a few weeks."

Alvin extended his hand, but Samuel stood his stance without returning the gesture. After a second, Alvin dropped his hand and focused back on Emma. "We had a nice time today. Hopefully, we can do it again before you head home."

Emma moved back down the steps and picked up her bag, "Thank you again for letting me tag along."

Lynette moved in closer and whispered, "Everything okay?"

Emma squeezed her new friend's hand before saying. "It'll be fine." She waved them on and headed back up the stairs.

Lillian gathered up the empty glasses and headed inside. "I'll let you two catch up while I go start some supper."

Emma tilted her chin toward her husband. "That was pretty rude of you, don't you think? Alvin was only trying to be friendly." Samuel sat back down and grasped the arms of the wicker rocker. The muscles in his jaw quivered, and a bead of sweat rolled down his forehead.

There was no question about it; her comment only added fuel to the fire. She moved the chair closer and laid her hand across his knee. "I know you're upset with me, and you have every right to be."

She followed his glare to Alvin and Lynette walking down the middle of the street. He wiped a bead of sweat from his brow and her heart took on a new rhythm as a shade of red rose from his neck. He jerked his knee away, forcing her hand to fall.

"I thought you were dead in a snowbank somewhere."

"Samuel, please ...I tried to call as soon as I got here."

"You had no right coming all this way without clearing it with me first."

Emma folded her hands in her lap and blew out a long breath. "I know."

Samuel stood and moved toward the steps. "I need to clear my head." He didn't look back as he followed the sidewalk to the street.

Tears pooled on Emma's bottom lashes as the blurred view of Samuel walking away clouded her vision. The disappointment was evident in his slumped shoulders, and she debated whether she should run after him. No matter how much she wanted to erase the last ten weeks, it would take more than one short conversation to ease the hurt they both experienced. For a minute, she questioned his love for her. If he loved her as much as he always claimed, wouldn't it be easier for him to forgive her? But instead, he once again chose to flee when things got tough.

Lillian opened the door. "Supper is just about ready."

"I don't think I have much of an appetite."

"Emma, you have to eat. And Samuel, he must be starving after his long ordeal on his way here." She stepped out on the porch and looked around the yard. "Where did he go? Is he looking at the bushes along the side of the house that I mentioned need trimmed?"

Emma wiped the moisture from her eyes with the back of her hand. "He went for a walk."

Lillian stood at her side and tenderly patted her shoulder. "He'll come around."

"I don't think so, he's pretty mad."

"According to Mary, he couldn't run to the bus stop fast enough to find you at the beach. To me, that's a man in love. Let him figure things out in his own head first, then he'll be ready to talk."

"He went to Siesta Beach?"

"He sure did, but he wasn't gone but a couple of hours after Mary had dropped off his coat and bag. I assumed he couldn't find you and headed back."

"He sat in that chair all day waiting for you to come home. Didn't say but a handful of words. Just sat there all afternoon with the sun beating on his face."

Emma shook her head. "Oh, *Mommi*, I'm not sure how we're ever going to get through this."

Lillian moved to the railing. "I learned many years ago grief knits two hearts together more than any amount of happiness ever can. Men need to sort things out inside. If he went for a walk, he's doing exactly that. When he comes back, he will have calmed down and be ready to face you."

"We're having so much trouble communicating. I have things I need to explain, but every time I try, we end up arguing."

Lillian moved to the rocker next to her. "Perhaps you both need to talk to someone."

"He would never agree to that."

"Have you asked him?"

"No. I thought maybe Alvin and Lynette might be able to help."

Lillian leaned over and rested her hand on Emma's arm. "I think they are exactly what you both need. Spend some time with those two and you'll both go back to Pennsylvania different people."

"How so?"

Lillian smiled before patting her arm again. "Let's just say I've seen it happen before. They're on a mission for the Lord and typically find ways to change people's lives every time they come to Pinecraft."

Her grandmother changed the subject. "So, did you have a good time with them today?"

"I did. Did you know they lost a child too?"

"Mary mentioned that. How is she doing?"

"They both seem to be handling it much better than Samuel and I."

Lillian pushed a strand of gray hair back under her *kapp*. "I'm not surprised."

"Well, let me go finish supper. If you change your mind, I'll keep a plate on the back of the stove for you. Martha's making brownies for dessert. Maybe that will spike Samuel's appetite when he returns."

Emma whispered under her breath. "If he returns."

Pushing herself from the chair, Emma grabbed her beach bag and carried it inside. The smells coming from the kitchen did little to entice her to eat. Instead, she headed to her bedroom for a change of clothes.

Samuel's duffle bag and winter coat sat on the end of the bed. She picked up his jacket and brought it to her nose. The smell of wood and horse filled her senses as she breathed in her husband. She wrapped herself in his coat and curled up in a ball in the center of the bed and thought, *how had they come so far, only to be so far apart?*

***

Samuel rested his foot on the railing at the shuffleboard court and watched four men push yellow pucks back and forth across the painted triangles on the green courts. Mesmerized by the slow slide of the disks, he didn't realize an older gentleman was speaking to him.

"I'm up next but my partner didn't show up. Want to play?"

Samuel looked over his shoulder, expecting to see someone behind him. "Me?"

"*Jah.*"

"Don't know the first thing about the game."

The man gestured for him to crawl over the fence. "You'll catch on quick."

Samuel hesitated but decided it would be better to play a round of shuffleboard rather than head back to face Emma.

The older man extended his hand. "Henry Mast."

Samuel firmly gripped his outstretched hand. "Samuel Yoder."

"Northwest Pennsylvania?"

"How'd you guess?"

"Your shirt and trousers gave it away. My brother owns a lumber mill in Willow Springs. Mast Lumber, do you know it?"

"How about I live a mile from it?"

"Nothing surprises me. We meet folks from all over the country down here. Most times, we find we're related in one way or another."

Samuel took off his heavy black hat and laid it on the bench behind him. He pushed his damp bangs out of his eyes and concentrated on the rules of the game as Henry explained them.

"I think I got it. The object is to move your puck in the scoring zone without going outside the lines."

"I knew you'd catch on quick."

As Samuel took his turn, Henry asked, "So what brings you to Pinecraft? Work or pleasure."

Samuel nodded his chin in Henry's direction as he used the long paddle, or what Henry called the pang, to propel his biscuit to the other end of the court. The yellow puck slid tightly into the eight-position, knocking one of their opponents' biscuits off the board. Henry slapped Samuel on the back. "I think I found myself a new partner!"

Samuel stood off to the side as Henry studied his next move and said, "Lucky shot."

"Lucky shot my foot. It takes most guys weeks to score like that."

Samuel enjoyed the friendly game for the next hour with little conversation other than a few sly remarks about his form and skill level.

After Henry made his last shot, he held up his paddle and said, "That's game, boys. Tomorrow at noon?"

The two men at the far end of the court waved and handed their pangs to the waiting players.

Henry and Samuel did the same and moved to the back of the court under the covered benches. "So how about it? Tomorrow at noon?"

Samuel took a drink from the cold-water bottle Henry pulled from the cooler before responding, "Maybe."

"I'll take that as a yes." Henry swung the canvas bag over his shoulder and walked to where his friends had gathered.

The sun started its descent over Phillippi Creek while Samuel sat viewing a volleyball game in progress. Before long, he'd have to make his way back to Emma's grandmother's house or choose to spend the night on one of the benches in the park. After his night on the steps, he needed a soft bed, regardless of how badly he didn't want to face the truth about Emma. Conflict, especially with his wife, was one thing he hoped he could avoid at all costs.

The short walk back to Graber Avenue did little to calm his apprehension. A slight breeze had cooled the evening temperature to a comfortable setting, and he took refuge back in the rocker on the porch. Off in the distance, someone played a harmonica, and the aroma of grilling meat floated through the air. His stomach growled, and he hoped he could find something to eat without disturbing Lillian or her *schwester*.

As if Emma read his mind, she appeared on the porch, plate in hand. "You missed dinner. Lillian made chicken and biscuits, one of your favorites."

She handed him the plate and set a glass of ice water on the stand between them. "*Denki*," was all he could muster.

"After you eat, can we talk?"

He wasn't in the mood for a lengthy conversation, but he was hungry and bowed his head for a silent prayer without answering her. He pushed a biscuit around on his plate and watched her out of the corner of his eye. In the two weeks, since they'd been apart, she changed. What it was, he couldn't pinpoint. Not yet back to herself, but not so rough around the edges. Maybe the brightly colored dress added color to her cheeks, or it was the day in the sun. Whatever it was, she looked rested. It could be that the time they spent apart transformed her, and if that was the case, he was at his wit's end to know how to fix it.

She calmly sat with her hands folded on her lap, waiting for him to finish without muttering a word. The silence almost drowned out the evening whispers of their surroundings. After taking the last bite, he balanced his plate on the railing in front of him and picked his glass back up. Clearing his throat without looking her way, he asked, "Where are your own clothes?"

She snapped her head in his direction. "We haven't seen each other in almost two weeks, and your only concern is my clothes?"

He took a drink before responding, "It's customary to honor our child for a year. I say your attire would hardly be considered such."

"You sound a lot like Bishop Weaver, and the last time I checked, he's over a thousand miles away."

"Regardless of how far we are from home, I'd prefer you follow our ways."

He knew his wife well enough to know the sudden rise and fall of her chest was an indication she was suppressing her words.

"We have more important things to discuss other than my clothes."

Samuel placed the glass on the table and stood near the railing with his back to her. "We do. Let's start with you going to the beach with Alvin."

"I didn't go alone. Lynette was with us."

"It's not proper."

Emma squeezed her fingers together. "Where's this coming from? You're being unreasonable."

Samuel glared. "Unreasonable? Let's talk about being irresponsible. How about taking off without letting me know where you were going? Or not calling. How about spending the day at the beach like you were on vacation or something?"

Emma looked over her shoulder to the window. "Lower your voice. *Mommi* hasn't gone to bed yet."

He clenched his jaw. "I don't really care who hears me. The fact is you're acting as if you have no responsibility to me or our life in Willow Springs."

"If I remember correctly, it was you who sent me off to my mother's when you didn't know what else to do with me. And you ...who shuts down whenever I want to talk about James. You care more about finishing that house than you do about how I'm feeling."

Samuel sat back down so hard the chair hit the gray stucco wall. "Because life goes on."

Emma sat up straight. "For you, but not me."

"What's that supposed to mean?"

"When life got hard, you pawned me off on someone else and then got mad when I changed course. You wanted me to find a way to deal with everything that happened. Well, this is the way I chose."

Samuel stayed quiet as she spoke to him in a tone unlike herself. Surer of herself and bolder than the Emma he'd known since before she could walk.

She stood and reached for the door. "We're getting nowhere, and I've had just about enough of this day. I'm going to bed."

Samuel stayed on the front porch long after the inside lights were put to sleep. He didn't handle any of it like a true leader of his family and so desperately wanted a do-over. They had been married for a little over a year, and he felt ill-equipped to handle such upheaval. One step forward and five back was the only thing mulling over in his head. There was no denying it; Emma was much better at expressing her feelings than he was. But again, he was a man and typically didn't have an emotion he could put into words. More than once, Emma asked him to express his feelings, but they were foreign to him. When she was broken and begging for his understanding, all he could say was ...*nothing* ...because nothing was typically what was in his head. What had his mother explained to him? ...*This is a season for her, and she must fight her way back in her own way, in her own time...* Could this be how she was fighting back? If it was, he didn't like it too much. But again, neither of them liked anything about the last few months.

Like always, he needed something to keep his hands busy. Instead of going inside, he walked off the porch and pulled the overhead roll-top door open to Martha's garage.

He found the chain to the overhead light and walked to the bench along the far wall. A broken bird feeder and half-painted porch sign filled the table. After several attempts to hammer the tiny pieces back together, he sat on a stool next to the workbench. Irritating bugs circled his head and landed on his sweat-filled face. It was past nine o'clock, and even though a slight breeze was evident, it did little to cool him off in the enclosed structure. He switched on a small fan on the table, and it blew the pesky bugs away from his face. If life could only be so easy, he'd flip a switch and blow the ugliness of the day away.

CHAPTER 12

The purr of the air conditioner woke Emma out of her restless sleep. The strange sounds and the illuminated alarm clock forced her to open her eyes. Light made its way through the blinds, just as a shift in the mattress alarmed her. She had no idea when Samuel came to bed, but a layer of uneasiness faded away, knowing he was at least by her side. She turned to face his sleeping features and missed the coziness they shared during the wee hours of the day. Oh, how she wished they could find their way back.

She gently crawled out of bed and moved slowly over the cool tile floor toward the door. Inviting smells lingered in the air as she made her way to the kitchen. Lillian sat at the table peeling apples and smiled at Emma when she poured herself a cup of coffee.

Without saying a word, Lillian pushed a flyer across the table with the point of her knife. "I asked Mary to drop off information about the group Alvin leads at the church. I thought perhaps you and Samuel might want to check it out."

Emma stirred sugar in her cup and picked up the brightly colored brochure. Printed across the top of the flyer was YOUR PERSONAL INVITATION TO MEET JESUS.

Emma flipped the paper over. *Come join us as we gather to glorify God through fellowship to study God's Word. The Bible provides practical answers to life's questions for all willing to listen and obey what it teaches. Enjoy a warm and friendly atmosphere where God's Word is clearly taught and discover the truth of Jesus.*

"*Mommi*, what do you think they mean by discover the truth of Jesus? I've heard that so many times over the last couple weeks."

Lillian peered over her wire-rimmed glasses she wore low on her nose. "Like I said yesterday, I believe you'll go home a different person, and in more ways than one if you spend some time with Alvin and Lynette."

Emma laid the brochure aside and picked back up her mug. "I have the feeling you're trying to tell me something. Can't you just come out and say it?"

Her grandmother continued to peel an apple and paused a few moments before continuing, "Sometimes, what you need to learn needs to grow deep inside your heart."

Emma picked up a slice of apple and nibbled on it before adding, "I'm starting to question bits and pieces of my life that make no sense."

Lillian asked, "Like what?"

"To begin with, why have Lynette and Alvin found it so easy to get over losing their child when Samuel and I are a mess?"

"I doubt they've gotten over it. I think they've ridden the storm through God's Word."

"You think they found comfort in the bible?"

"I do. Security you can only find deep in the chapters of Jesus' story."

Emma fidgeted in her chair. "Have you read the bible?"

"A few times. But it wasn't until I was in my fifties before I picked up an English version."

Emma raised an eyebrow. "Marie gave me hers when I visited."

Lillian popped a slice of apple in her mouth. "Have you started to read it yet?"

"No, I feel like I'm betraying Samuel. We are to read from the German Bible."

Lillian picked up a towel and dried her hands. "Emma, my dear, let me tell you a story about your birth father."

Emma rested her hands around her cup and leaned in. "Does it have anything to do with why he left the Amish in the first place?"

"That it does. What your grandfather told you years ago about him jumping the fence to the English world had little to do with the truth. Yes, he was drinking way too much. But he struggled to understand why our church leaders were so blind to what was clearly outlined in God's Word. He got in trouble for sharing what he read with the young folk around our community. Your birth mother, Marie, was Mennonite and knew the truth."

"I'm confused. What was my father sharing that was so bad it got him excommunicated?"

Lillian folded her hands over Emma's. "He shared the truth of salvation through Jesus Christ."

Emma flipped her hands over and squeezed her grandmother's soft fingers. "Stella left me a note. She spoke of the same thing. She told me I had to search for the truth of Jesus. How is it I've been taught that my only way to heaven was through my works, and I wouldn't learn if I made it to heaven until the day I stand before him?"

"Child, listen to me. Jesus died on the cross to pave your way to heaven, and the only way to get there is to accept Jesus Christ as your Lord and Savior deep in your heart. None of us will find our forever home through our works because none of us will ever be good enough."

"And the bible tells us this, are you sure?"

"I'm surer of it than I am of anything else on this earth."

Emma furrowed her eyebrows. "And my birth father left the Amish because of this?"

"He did. It wasn't until after he died that your grandfather and the other ministers chose to look for the truth on their own. It was your father's shunning that changed the way our leaders shared the Word. Because of your father, our whole community was encouraged to study a bible they understood."

"But *Mommi,* this isn't what Samuel and I were taught, and not what my *datt* believes." Emma brought her fingers to her lips and whispered, "I bet that's why *Datt* got so upset when I told him about *Mamm's* letter. He told me I shouldn't share it with anyone. It would cause too much turmoil in the community."

Lillian lowered her voice and nodded, "It will, for sure and certain."

Emma rested her chin in the palm of her hands. "Between James and this with Samuel, it's just way too much."

Lillian pointed to the flyer on the table. "One thing at a time. Go to the meeting. I'm certain it will help. Then the Lord will find a way to help you accept everything else."

"But what should I do about Samuel? He'll never agree with any of this. Just one more secret I'm keeping from him."

Noise in the hallway hushed them both, and Lillian tapped the brochure and mouthed, "Go."

Emma tucked the flyer in her housecoat pocket.

***

Samuel stood in the hallway, a few feet from the kitchen, and listened in on Emma and her grandmother's conversation. Once again, he heard Emma share things she should be telling him. What happened to the closeness they once had? Shouldn't a wife share things with her husband first? And what was the secret she was keeping from him? One more thing to put a wedge between them. With every passing day, they slipped farther and farther apart. How was he to keep their marriage from sinking?

Clearing his throat, he took the last few steps into the kitchen. He looked past Emma and nodded a warm good morning to Lillian.

Emma stood and rushed to the stove to pour him a cup of coffee. "Are you hungry? I could make you breakfast?"

He pressed his lips together and ran his hand through his hair. "No, just coffee."

All the air seemed to be sucked from the room with his icy response. Emma's tone sounded hopeful when she asked, "It's Christmas Eve, and Alvin invited us to come to their Christmas Eve service. Would you like to go?"

Even the sound of Alvin's name coming from Emma's lips forced his chest muscle to tense. "I have plans today."

"Plans? What might they be?"

His gut response was to lash out, but with Lillian in the room, he brought it down a level and responded, "I just have plans."

Lillian stood to leave. "Help yourself to anything you want; I'll take my coffee out to the front porch."

Samuel waited until Lillian closed the front door before addressing Emma.

"I checked the bus schedule, and the first seat available is next Wednesday. I assume you'll be ready to go home by then?"

Emma leaned against the counter. "There is a meeting next Wednesday night at the church. I was hoping you'd go with me."

"We don't need a meeting; we need to go home."

"Samuel, please. Maybe you don't think you do, but I do."

Samuel leaned over to tie his boot. "What you need to do is move on. God has made it clear James was not ours to keep. We've been over this; how many more times do we need to discuss it?"

Emma laid her hand across his arm. "It's not just James. I have questions, and I think I can only get my answers if we stay in Pinecraft a bit longer. I think Alvin might be able to help us."

The vein at his temple bulged. "What is it about him that you keep bringing his name into our problems?"

"He's a minister, and I think he can help."

"What do you think Bishop Weaver is? I'm sure he would be willing to answer any questions we have. He even told me so before I left."

Samuel folded up his shirt sleeves while she asked, "Told you what?"

"That we might have questions, and we weren't to be ashamed if we did."

Emma played with the hem of her housecoat. "I have things I need to sort out, but I don't think Bishop Weaver can help me with any of them."

In a gruff tone, he replied, "I feel like we're playing cat and mouse. How about you share your questions with me and let me decide if we need to bring them before the bishop."

Emma found a tissue in her pocket and rolled it through her fingers. "We have to sort through a few things, but I need to talk to someone who can help me get past this block I have with God."

He pushed his chair away from the table and towered over her. "Then you'll do it alone. Next Wednesday, I'm leaving for home, with or without you."

The back door slammed shut, and he only glanced back for a moment. Emma's pretty eyes turned dark, and one more layer of distress inched its way between them.

Heading to the garage, a loose sheet of paper blew across the yard in front of him. Stomping his foot on top of the flyer, he picked it up and read the bold letters. *YOUR PERSONAL INVITATION TO MEET JESUS – Come to the picnic shelter at Pinecraft Park on Saturday at 2:00 pm to find out more.* He folded the paper and stuffed it in his pocket before opening the garage door.

***

The sting of Samuel's words weighed heavy on Emma's heart. She placed their cups in the sink and went to get dressed. Everything in her grandmother's house was strange. Even though they still reverted to reading by lantern, everything else in the small cottage screamed English. Both Lillian and Martha told her they indulged in a few more liberties in Pinecraft than in Sugarcreek. She couldn't help but think for once in her life, it would be Pinecraft's liberty that would allow her to explore things her strict Old Order community forbids. For that she felt hopeful.

She opened the dresser drawer and uncovered Marie's bible. The well-worn leather felt smooth in her hands, and she fanned the pages through her fingers. There was no doubt about it. She was about to embrace a new chapter in her life. Deep inside, she struggled to figure out if she was feeling fear or the anticipation of something bigger.

The hair on her arms tingled, and she stopped at the place where Marie's bookmark was tucked in its spine. She read the words from the card over again. *IF YOU SENSE YOUR FAITH IS UNRAVELLING* ...and whispered to herself, "Is that what I'm feeling, my faith unraveling?"

She scanned through the thin pages looking for something, but she didn't know what. Her grandmother wouldn't tell her something that wasn't true, neither would Stella or Marie. She had to find the truth, but where to start.

Samuel's deep voice echoed through the walls, and she scurried to hide Marie's bible under the layer of clothes while his footsteps came closer. She took a yellow dress from the drawer and laid it on the bed just as he opened the door.

He glared at the brightly colored fabric and snarled, "I forgot my hat."

She picked it up from the top of the dresser and handed it to him. He held one side and her the other, neither wanting to break the line between them. "I'll be securing bus tickets today, for next Wednesday."

She dropped her hold on the hat. "I'm not going home yet."

The lines in his jaw protruded, and he turned and walked away.

Emma sat down on the bed and ran her hand across the lightweight dress. If he couldn't come to terms with her wanting to stay, how was he ever going to accept her need to find the truth her mother's spoke of? Or even the issue of them not having children for two years? She laid back on the unmade bed and tucked her legs under the quilt. All she wanted to do was hide under the covers and scream.

***

The small wooden bird feeder fell apart in Samuel's hand when he added more pressure to the flimsy sides than necessary. Emma's defiance frustrated him to no end, and the dull pain behind his eyes magnified every time he pictured the yellow dress.

Samuel felt his presence long before Henry Mast said a word. "Mary Miller said I'd find you here. I wanted to make sure I still had a partner today."

The birdhouse tumbled in pieces in front of him, and Samuel groaned, "Ugh."

Henry stepped off his bike and moved beside him. "Glue would probably work better."

Samuel dug around on the shelf above his head for a bottle of wood glue. "These big hands were meant for farming and framing, not projects like this."

Henry leaned on the workbench. "Young men like you find it hard to sit still down here. Not enough to do, they say."

"I'd have to agree with them. If I could, I'd be on a bus heading home by now."

"Why so fast? You just got here. I'd say by the looks of that feeder, you need to unwind some."

Samuel took a pair of pliers to loosen the cap to the glue. "*Jah*, I made a mess of it."

"Spend some time with us old folks, and the cares of the world won't seem so big."

Samuel put the cap to the bottle aside. "I could only wish."

Henry held the side and bottom of the feeder together as Samuel trailed a glue line along the edge. "Whatever's eating at you is probably not as big as you're making it."

Samuel added a clamp to hold the wood together. "Women."

Henry laughed and said, "Well, that explains it all. When women are involved, I throw all advice out the window."

Samuel picked up a red rag and wiped the glue from his fingers. "Do I need to say more?"

Henry stepped back over his bike, sat on the seat, and used his feet to push it backwards out of the garage. "All I can say is listen."

"Listen?"

"*Jah*, listen. We're hard-headed, and if we listen, instead of trying to find a way to fix things, messes like that bird feeder wouldn't happen."

Henry's words didn't really make sense, but he pushed them aside momentarily as Henry made his way down the driveway. "Noon?"

"Probably."

"Good, and remember you can't fix everything, but you can listen."

Glue was no longer on Samuel's hands, but he continued to run the rag over his fingers while he thought, *It's my job to fix things. I've been listening, but all I've heard is her talking to everyone but me.*

Shaking his head, he moved to the back of the garage in search of hedge trimmers. If he couldn't fix his wife, he could at least take care of some things around the house.

He stuffed the shop rag in his pocket and stopped when the piece of paper touched his fingers. Pulling the flyer from his pocket, he reread the invitation. YOUR PERSONAL INVITATION TO MEET JESUS. Maybe he'd stick around the park for the afternoon to see what it was all about.

CHAPTER 13

E mma hadn't meant to fall back asleep and only woke when Lillian stood over her.

"Emma, Lynette is here. Should I tell her you're resting?"

Brushing her hair from her face, she asked, "What time is it?"

"It's eleven-thirty."

"Oh my, I slept all morning. Please tell Lynette I'll be right out." Emma reached out to grab her grandmother's sleeve. "I'm sorry you had to listen to Samuel and me this morning."

Lillian touched her hand. "No worries, you're both young, and you'll find a way to work through your differences. I'm sure of it. I think what you need to do is spend some time with Lynette. Both she and Alvin have helped a good many of the

205

young folk around here, and I'm sure they can help you and Samuel as well."

In a hopeful plea she said, "I sure hope so."

"Trust me, child, if you'll both open your hearts to what they have to share, you'll find the peace you need."

"I sure hope so, *Mommi*."

"Now get dressed, and I'll make Lynette some tea while she's waiting."

Lynette and her grandmother had moved to the front porch and were murmuring when she found them. As she opened the door, she heard her grandmother say. "She needs a friend like you."

Emma stepped outside and said, "I do need a friend, that's for sure."

Lynette stood. "Good because I could use a friend to join me at the Coffee Café."

Emma kissed her grandmother on the cheek before saying, "That sounds like a great idea."

Both girls stepped off the porch and waved at Lillian as they headed to the street.

Lynette grabbed Emma's arm to slow down. "Not so fast, we have all day, and there is no reason to rush."

Emma fell into step with her. "I'm sorry I forgot I don't have a list of chores I need to complete. Not that I've been doing many chores lately, I've spent more time sulking around than anything constructive the last couple months."

"I totally agree, but here in Pinecraft, we can indulge in a slower pace."

They walked for a few minutes without saying a word until Emma asked, "My grandmother said you and Alvin help the young folk around here. What do you do?"

"Well, Alvin does a good bit, but all I do is help him wherever I can."

"Like what?"

Lynette pulled a flyer from her purse and handed it to her. "Come see for yourself."

"*Mommi* showed me that flyer this morning. I want to go, but I'm not sure I can convince Samuel to come. He wants to go home on Wednesday."

"Emma, you have to come, and hopefully, we can get Samuel to agree too. It will do you both some good. Alvin is a great teacher. He has gone through training and has a way of helping our people through tough spots by looking to the Bible for answers."

Emma held the flyer up to study it closer. "So what does he teach about?"

"All sorts of things. But mainly, we show you how to turn to Jesus for answers."

Emma handed the brochure back to Lynette and asked, "Do you believe God puts us on a path for a reason?"

"Do I ever. I think you got on that bus in Sugarcreek because he paved your way to Pinecraft. I don't think it was a coincidence that you and I met, and Samuel followed you here. Both of you were meant to hear what Alvin and I have to say. I'm sure of it."

"How can you be so sure?"

"Because you're not the first young couple from an Old Order community that has crossed our path. God lines Alvin and me up with young couples all the time. Most times, they have an issue they need to talk through just like you and Samuel do."

"You sound so confident. How can you be so sure Samuel and I were meant to be here?"

"The good Lord gave Alvin the gift of teaching, and he uses it to open the eyes of many people to the love of Jesus."

Both girls stopped talking long enough to order drinks and find a free table under an umbrella. Once they settled into their seats, Emma continued, "I have to tell you I feel something huge is going to shift in my life. I can't pinpoint what it is, but I'm excited and fearful at the same time."

Lynette smiled. "Emma, you have no idea what's about to happen, but by the grace of God, you will come to understand how trusting in Jesus will change your life; if you'll let Him."

A nervous giggle escaped Emma's lips. "You're scaring me."

Lynette laughed and stirred her drink with the straw. "Trust me, you have nothing to fear. Once you fully understand how Jesus walks with you and you truly trust Him in everything. Your fear will turn into a passion like nothing you've ever experienced."

Emma sat back in her chair and wiped the moisture from the outside of her cup. "But we still have one obstacle."

"What's that?"

"Samuel. He's ready to go home."

Lynette grinned. "I'm not going to worry about that, and neither should you. God will take care of that, I'm sure of it."

"He's pretty set on going home, with or without me, were his exact words."

"Have faith Emma. God works all things for His good, and that includes helping Samuel see how much you both need what we want to share."

Emma tried to embrace Lynette's confidence, but she knew her husband. If he thought they were going against the *Ordnung,* he'd never agree, or that was what she assumed.

Emma changed the subject, hoping to push away her apprehension of Samuel agreeing to stay in Pinecraft longer. "Can I ask you something?"

"Sure, what is it?"

"I know you're still hurting from your own loss, but you don't seem to wear it on your sleeve as obviously as I do. How are you doing that?"

"You can't see it, can you?"

"No, what is it?"

"If I hadn't lost a child just like you, I wouldn't have been led to reach out to you on the bus. You would have slipped right by me without any connection, and we most likely wouldn't be sitting here right now. How can that not be from God?"

Emma opened her hands and waved them through the air. "So, you're saying all of this was to bring us together?"

"I'm certain of it."

Lynette leaned in and whispered, "Look around. All of these people have come from an array of communities. Old Order, New Order, Beachy Amish, and Mennonite. Pinecraft is a melting pot of different beliefs all in one place. Young and old. Believers of salvation through works and believers of salvation through Christ. What better place to spread God's word than right here in Pinecraft? It's no accident you and Samuel are here, and it's no accident we both lost a child to bring us together."

Emma laid a hand on her heart. "I'm still mad at God for taking James and not allowing me to have more children right away."

"He has a bigger plan for you, Emma Yoder. You just can't see it yet. But I promise you before you leave Florida, you'll figure out what that might be."

"Do you have any idea what it is?"

"I have a few thoughts, but that's between you and God, and I'll let Him show you in His own time."

Lynette threw her cup in the trash. "How about we walk to the Park? The old guys should be playing shuffleboard by now, and it's fun to watch."

***

Samuel showed up a few minutes before noon and not one minute before Henry was about to send out a search party. Rounding the corner of the pavilion Henry hollered, "It's about time."

"I had a run-in with a hedge trimmer."

"I entered us into a tournament next Wednesday. Our start time is two, and we are players eight and nine."

Samuel threw his shoulders back. "I was thinking about heading home on Wednesday."

"I don't think so," Henry added as he handed Samuel the paddle.

Samuel picked up the pang and made his first shot. "What makes you so sure?"

"Because you have a tournament to play in, and what's so pressing at home other than shoveling snow?"

Samuel didn't answer but gave the old man a pointed look.

The two played the rest of the game with barely a word between them. When Henry guided the biscuit to the other end of the court, they both hollered when his shot won the game. "See, another reason why you're not going home on Wednesday. That win just moved us up to the next level. We go up against the winning team from last year. No way I'm looking for a new player this late in the season."

Samuel pushed his bangs off his forehead, "Good thing I didn't buy tickets yet, or you'd have no choice but to find another player."

Henry slapped Samuel on the back. "The Lord knows what he's doing, I'm sure of it."

"I'm not so sure a Shuffleboard Tournament is high on his priority list."

"We'll see about that; you can count on it."

"I'm not counting on anything but finding something cold to drink and getting out of this sun."

They handed the pangs off to the following players and walked to a shaded picnic bench. Henry handed him a bottle of water. "There is the team we go up against next week. I think I'll sit right here and see if I can figure out their strategy."

Samuel let out a deep snort. "Strategy? Not so sure there's much skill or advanced planning to push a disk around."

"Maybe so, but let's watch just in case."

Samuel looked up under the picnic shelter, hoping to see some signs of the meeting he wanted to catch, before taking a seat beside Henry.

"Looking for someone?"

Samuel pulled the flyer out of his pocket and showed it to Henry. "Do you know what this is all about?"

"Ah, *jah*. Alvin Miller preaches, and he and his wife Lynette facilitate a bible study. They visit us a few times a year and do an excellent job reaching out to the community while they're here.

"His wife?"

"*Jah*, Lynette. Sweet girl. I hear they lost a baby a few months back, and I was surprised she joined him this time."

Like a freight train, Samuel felt his harsh treatment slap him in his face. "Alvin's a minister?"

"Sure is, and one of the best around, in my books. He might be young, but he's got the voice of God running through his veins."

"How so?"

214

"Come find out for yourself."

Henry studied Samuel's face before asking, "You're in the same church district as my brother in Willow Springs?"

"*Jah.*"

He made a sound Samuel couldn't quite understand and then Henry asked, "You never did answer what brought you to Pinecraft."

Samuel swirled his hat on his finger and concentrated on the game at the other end of the court. He had no desire to share with Henry the real reason he came to Pinecraft.

Henry stood. "Whatever the reason, I guarantee you'll go home a different man if you stick around a while."

"How so?"

"Take my word for it. You'll see soon enough, I'm sure."

Samuel didn't like puzzles, and Henry's vague warning didn't sit quite right. Following voices from the group, gathering at the far end of the shelter Samuel turned on the bench. He looked at the flyer one more time and crumbled it and threw it in the trash. Something drew him to the crowd, and he waited until his eyes adjusted to the shade before finding a seat near the front.

***

Lynette and Emma stopped at the fence to watch a game in progress before following a group to the covered shelter. "Alvin is going to talk briefly about our meeting on Wednesday night. Let's go listen."

Emma looked ahead and grabbed Lynette's arm. "Samuel's here."

"Where?"

Emma pointed and whispered, "Right there."

"Do you want to go sit with him?"

Emma stopped walking and contemplated what she should do. "No, I don't think so. I want to hear what Alvin has to say, but I'm not sure Samuel would want me to know he's here. He told me he had plans today. Maybe this was what he was referring to."

She pulled Lynette back. "Let's sit back here, so he doesn't see me.

Emma watched as her husband leaned his elbows on his knees and twirled his hat around his fingers; something he did when he was uncomfortable. She closed her eyes and said a silent prayer hoping God would lay something on his heart that would soften his stance about leaving so soon.

A couple dozen people gathered around Alvin and waited for him to begin. Emma wiped her palms on the skirt of her dress and took a seat beside Lynette. A pillar blocked Samuel from her view, and she shielded herself further behind Lynette's shoulder.

Alvin cleared his throat and began. "Who here likes to play baseball?"

Almost everyone under the shelter held their hand up. Samuel, however, kept his head hung low.

"I like to use the game as a metaphor for meeting Jesus. In a game, we all come together to play as a team. Every position is important, and no one can play without relying on each team member to play his part. Agree?"

Everyone nodded in agreement.

"So, who here thinks life has thrown them a curve ball?"

Alvin nodded his head in the direction of those who held their hands up. "Who here would like to think they had someone in their corner to pinch-hit when life threw them out of the game?" Again, just about everyone raised their hand.

Alvin smiled before saying, "Me too!"

"If you showed up here today, then it's your first step in discovering the truth in Jesus and getting in the game."

"First, let me explain. I know how difficult it might be to admit you have something in your life throwing you out. It could be a job, relationship issues, the loss of a loved one, and yes, even addiction. Whatever you're struggling with can be addressed if you put your trust in Jesus for your salvation and have faith you'll make it home through Him."

A sudden hum of whispers filtered around the group. The air under the picnic shelter stopped, and many attendees looked at Alvin, hoping he'd explain further. By the looks of the people who had gathered, many were Old Order and had little knowledge of Jesus's actual plan for their lives. Yes, they believed He existed and would meet Him if they worked hard enough to follow the rules. But trust him in salvation? That was foreign to their ears. Emma cringed when Samuel spoke up. "Many of us were not taught such things. Are you certain you want to expose these young people to these teachings? You do realize what upheaval it will cause to their families."

"Good question and I bet many of you have the same concern. Our Wednesday night Bible study is a tool to help you move forward in your walk with Jesus. Which, in turn, will help you maneuver your way around the bases of ensuring you make it to your forever home. You can only know what God offers us if you study the bible in greater detail."

Emma's sensed Samuel's jaw tense even if she couldn't see his face. She thought for sure he was about to leave, but he settled back down as Alvin continued.

"What I'm trying to share is that there are many scriptures that have been kept from you. A truth that can only be found when you look deep in the pages of the bible. A truth that will set you free. What I'm about to share will cause an awakening in your heart that may change your life forever." Alvin held a bible above his head and asked, "How many of you have read this book?" A few young girls raised their hands but quickly put them down when everyone turned their way. Alvin smiled and continued, "There's no shame in admitting you've found yourself drawn to the pages of this book. It's the one place where you can find many answers to the questions you have and the one place where you'll find comfort like no other. The place where you'll find Jesus."

Emma bumped Lynette with her shoulder. "Samuel's going to flee. I can see how uneasy he is."

Lynette touched her arm. "Relax, let him finish. You'll be surprised at how he can draw people in."

"I'm not here to tell you I have all the answers, but I am here to say you don't have to go it alone. Life is hard, and things can be challenging, but I know of something bigger that can work in my life and yours. If you have something weighing you down, I invite you to join us on Wednesday evening. I promise to answer all of your questions then."

Emma sunk down when Samuel stood and spoke up. "You're asking many of these people to go against their church."

Alvin didn't back down and directed his following comment to Samuel. "I certainly understand your apprehension, and you have every right to question what I'm saying. But don't you owe it to yourself and your family to know the truth?"

In a huff, Samuel added, "You're setting these young people up for conflict within their own community."

"You're correct, it may. But studying the Word will help restore their faith in God, and they have major choices to make in their walk with Jesus. As followers of Christ, we aren't called to stand on the sidelines but to suit up and get in the game. "

Emma crawled under the picnic table. Her heart was about to burst out of her chest when Samuel's voice got louder as he stomped by. "You're just asking for trouble."

Emma watched as her husband's heavy boots passed by the table while she stayed hidden.

CHAPTER 14

Lillian and Martha moved in harmony around the kitchen, putting supper on the table. Their lighthearted chatter filled the air despite Emma trying to pull Samuel out of his solemn mood. He had no idea she witnessed his outburst earlier, and she prayed she could find a way to ease the surrounding tension.

Lillian filled his glass with ice water and asked, "Martha and I are going to the Christmas Eve service at the Mennonite Church. Would you and Emma like to go with us?"

Emma held her breath, waiting for him to respond. "I don't think it would be wise for us to attend but thank you for the invitation."

She knew it would cause a great deal of strife between them even before she said, "I want to go."

Lines etched around Samuel's eyes. "Bishop Weaver wouldn't approve"

A million thoughts rang through her head, but the one thing that gnawed at her soul was that her husband cared more about keeping face with the bishop than he did about learning the truth. On the other hand, she needed to find the peace and joy Lynette and Alvin carried with them, regardless of the cost.

Lillian put a casserole dish in the center of the table. "If you change your mind, it starts at seven."

Emma pushed potatoes and ham around on her plate as she tried to come up with the words needed to convince her husband to change his mind. There were times like this when she wished she could be more like her best friend, Katie. She would never go against Daniel in matters like this. Completely and without a doubt, Katie followed Daniel's lead in every aspect of their life. Katie was a much better Amish wife than she was.

No doubt about it, she had a mind of her own and often challenged Samuel in matters where he was to make the decisions. He often teased her that she favored her birth mother far more than she did her Amish *mamm*. This was one of those times when she knew she had to go against his wishes and follow her heart.

After Lillian and Martha excused themselves to the front room, Emma poured Samuel a cup of coffee and finished cleaning up the kitchen. Samuel sat at the head of the table reading through the Budget Newspaper. Words toyed around in Emma's head until she said, "I don't mean to go against your wishes, and I certainly don't want to upset you more than you are already, but I feel I have to go tonight."

He snapped the paper and lowered it below his chin, "What do you want from me? How can I lead us if you argue with me about everything?"

In a tone that resembled hopelessness, he continued, "I'm really at my wit's end. I suppose I can't stop you if you want to go, but I'll not be joining you, and I will be bringing this up with the bishop when we return home."

For a moment, Emma sympathized with him, until he brought the bishop back up. "If I have to hear one more time about what Bishop Weaver thinks one more time, I'll go crazy. Since when do you hold on to his every word for guidance? Maybe Alvin is right. Don't you owe it to yourself and our family to know the truth?"

Samuel laid the paper aside. "Where were you this afternoon?"

"In the park, just like you."

"I don't need some young Mennonite preacher to tell me how I should lead my family and what I should be reading in scripture."

Lowering her voice Emma said, "Exactly why I felt drawn to him and what he has to say."

"Something is telling me I need to find out what Alvin is talking about. Samuel, I want to study the bible, but I can't do that at home. Please come with me. There has to be a reason God brought us here."

For a moment, she thought he might concede. His eyes darted around the room then settled on hers. "It goes against everything we've been taught. How can you expect me to throw twenty-three years of instruction out the window? Once you pick up that Bible, all things will change."

Emma rubbed her fingers across his forearm. "How can that be a bad thing?"

"Because we made a promise to God and our community to follow the ways of our forefathers."

"But Samuel, we're encouraged to look for instruction in the Bible. How can that go against anything we've been taught?

I want to know everything. I can't explain it, but I have a feeling God is trying to show us something."

Samuel leaned back in his chair and squared his shoulders, "I'm certain the ministers will tell us anything we want to know."

She gave him a few minutes to ponder his thoughts before adding, "I'm not so sure they'll tell us everything." She stood and said, "Wait here, I want to show you something."

Emma went to her room to find the letter Stella had left for her. Within seconds, she returned and removed the letter from the pink envelope and handed it to him.

Her pulse quickened when his expression didn't change, and he handed it back to her. "This truth your *mamm* speaks of will change us."

"So, you know what she's talking about? Why haven't you shared it with me? For weeks I've been trying to figure out what it means. Marie told me about it, Nathan's mother Rosie spoke of it. Lynette has been hinting about it, and even *Mommi* talks about salvation through Christ. Why haven't we been taught that?"

He stood and moved to the backdoor. "You need to drop it. I don't think either one of us is ready to face the turmoil this will cause."

"Samuel, please, I feel like we were sent here for a reason. This has to be God's answer for taking James from us. He wants us to learn the truth. Why else would he pave the way for us to come all the way to Pinecraft?"

There was a heaviness in the way Samuel opened the door. "You're asking for trouble for sure and certain."

When the door closed, Emma folded her arms on the table, rested her head in their creases, and prayed. "*Please, Lord, show me what you want me to do. I know going against my husband is not what you have in store for me. But I need to know what everyone is trying to teach me. They all can't be wrong, can they?*"

***

Samuel followed the street until he made his way back to Pinecraft Park. The path along the banks of Phillippi Creek called to him, and he maneuvered his way around a group of young men deep in a heated conversation about Alvin's earlier meeting.

"If my *datt* finds out, he'll put a stop to it right quick."

"Mine too. But what if that preacher is right?"

"My folks are pressuring me to take my kneeling vow, but before I do, I want to know the whole truth."

One of the boys hollered toward Samuel. "Hey, you were there this afternoon. What do you think? Is he right?"

Without answering right away, Samuel played his response over in his head. Had someone told him the truth before he promised God and his community to live by the rules of the *Ordnung,* he might have chosen otherwise. But now, he had no other choice but to abide by the rules he promised to uphold. Could he help this group of young men not make the same mistake?

He turned to face the group. "If you haven't already been baptized, I'd say you owe it to yourself to find the truth and then make your own decision."

His comment left the boys speechless, and he walked away.

There was no hesitation in speaking what he knew was real to the young boys. He knew what the truth would do to their lives, and it wasn't too late for them. But for him, it meant division and separation from his family. Hard as he might try, he knew he couldn't keep Emma from the truth much longer. He felt it the minute he heard Alvin speak. Emma wasn't the only one that was keeping secrets. He'd kept his bible reading from her for the past year and found himself sneaking away to read the words printed in English as often as he could. He knew she thought he accepted God's will to take James, but all along, Samuel knew God had bigger plans. It wasn't until the eager faces of the young people gathered under the picnic shelter that God revealed His plan.

He knew what he had to do, and that was to come clean with Emma. In his attempt to keep them from facing excommunication, he made Emma feel like their current strife was her fault. But in retrospect, it was his way of keeping them safe. But is that what God wanted him to do? He knew for a fact Emma was correct. God did bring them to Pinecraft for a reason, and that was to push him into revealing his true beliefs to Emma; to find the strength to step out in faith and go against everything he'd been taught. Even if it meant they would become outcasts from everyone and everything they held so dear.

As he sat on the banks of the creek, he opened his heart to God in a way he never had. It was time to be the true leader of his family and show Emma what Daniel had shown him so many months ago. To teach her the meaning of being a Christian was more than following a set a rules and outward appearances. It was laying her whole life at His feet and trusting He would guide her every step. All at once a wind blew across the waters of Phillippi Creek and he knew his old life was to be never more. A new life had been given to him regardless of what trouble it would cause when they returned to Willow Springs.

***

Emma sat on the edge of the bed and combed out her waist-length hair before coiling it up at the base of her neck. Taking a clean *kapp* from the top of the dresser, she pinned it in place and prayed Samuel wouldn't be too mad she disobeyed him.

Lillian knocked lightly on the door before pushing it open, "Are you sure you want to go with us? It might cause more trouble between the two of you."

"I have to go. Do you think I'm wrong?"

"I can't say one way or another, but we are to follow the lead of our husbands; the Bible tells us that."

Emma sat back down on the bed and asked, "Did you ever go against *Doddi* Melvin?"

Lillian sat down beside her. "Did I ever. And for this exact reason. When he and the other ministers refused to seek the truth about salvation, I questioned him. Your father showed me in his English Bible where God told us that we will be saved not by our works but through faith. Melvin was angry with me for a long time. He was certain if we read from the English bible, we would surely be misled."

"But you continued to search for the truth, didn't you?"

"What I did was continued to ask Melvin to prove to me that what we'd been taught was right. After months of him looking for answers, he finally admitted he couldn't prove your father was wrong."

Emma moved to the edge of the mattress and picked up her grandmother's hands. "You gave me an idea. You and Martha go without me. I need to find Samuel."

Lillian squeezed her fingers. "Good girl, go to your husband and work through it together. I'm certain God will show you what you need to do if you only listen."

Emma went to the dresser and pulled Marie's bible from beneath a stack of clothes. "Can you show me in the bible where God tells us about salvation through Christ?"

"I don't need to find it; I know exactly where it is. Read Ephesians Chapter 2: verses 8 and 9."

Emma snapped her head back in surprise. Chapter 2, 8, and 9?"

Lillian looked at her quizzically, "*Jah*, why?"

"Ever since I got here, those numbers keep showing up. Everywhere I turn, I see two, eight, and nine."

Lillian smiled before saying, "I'm not surprised. God never ceases to reveal things to us He wants us to see."

Emma kissed her grandmother on the cheek, picked up her mother's bible, and ran out the door. It had to be a sign from God; it just had to be.

***

After making his way back to Pinecraft Park, Samuel sat beneath a large oak tree covered in moss. A group of young people sat under the shade of the picnic shelter singing. The slow and drawn-out songs from home soothed his soul.

Tomorrow was Christmas, and all hopes of spending it in their new home were as far away as the miles that separated them. After hearing Alvin speak, he understood that what he overheard that day at the beach and then later at Emma's grandmother's house was a misunderstanding. He was just as guilty at keeping secrets as she was. He refused to admit it, but he had questions too; and that forced Emma to think he held Bishop Weaver's position higher than the Lord's. But all in all, he used the bishop as a cover for his own sin of not being honest with her.

"Samuel, can I sit with you?"

Startled by Emma's arrival, he followed her voice. The light green dress she wore made her features sparkle in the sun illuminated behind her head. Her big brown eyes were filled with love as she pointed to the spot in the grass next to him. "I think we need to talk."

He cleared a twig in the grass and held out his hand to help her sit. Energy sparked between them when their fingers touched. "I'm sorry," he whispered.

"No, I'm sorry I caused so much tension between us. I should have never come here without you, and I should have gone home."

He closed his eyes and took in a deep breath through his teeth before exhaling. "God called us here. I know that now."

She laid the bible down in the grass and turned to face him. "You feel it too?"

"I do, but there's something I need to explain first."

Emma folded her hands on her lap and lowered her chin. "No, me first. I kept something from you that I need to tell you before we go any further."

He didn't say a word and gave her the time she needed to compile her words. "First, I have to explain to you how mad I was at God for the last couple of months. I thought I must have done something wrong, or we must have not followed the rules well enough, and we were being punished."

He picked her fingers up and rubbed small circles over the back of her hand. "That's not true; God doesn't punish us like that. And believe me when you mentioned that before, I had to look for the truth myself."

"You did? Did you talk to Bishop Weaver?"

He picked up the bible and moved it to his lap. "No, I looked here."

"Did you find the answer in the bible? What does it say?"

"That bad things often happen so the works of God might be displayed."

"So, Lynette was right. She said things often happen so God can set us up for something bigger. Like me and her meeting, and Alvin sharing with us the true meaning of salvation with us."

"*Jah.*"

Emma sat up straight. "Wait, you read the bible? An English version?"

"*Jah.*"

"But why didn't you share it with me?"

"I couldn't. How could I encourage you to go against the promises you made? If word got out, we would be excommunicated or be made to go before the church to repent. I couldn't subject you to that. You were going through so much already."

"Is this what you wanted to tell me? Why have you been against me going to a bible study if you have questions yourself?"

He picked both of her hands up and turned to face her. "Emma, do you realize what will happen when we return home? If the bishop gets word of this, we'll not be able to see our families. We will be exiled in our own community. Is that what you want?"

Tears teetered on her bottom lashes. "I want to follow God's word. How can that be wrong?"

He reached up and pulled her face to his and rested his forehead on hers. "There will be no going back, you understand that, right?"

"What other choice do we have?"

"Believe me, I have tried to find a way around it for the last couple of weeks. I keep asking myself what I want to teach our *kinner.*"

Emma pulled her head away and put distance between them, but he pulled her close again. "Emma, we'll have more children, I'm sure of it."

"There may not be more. I've kept something from you. Something I should have told you a long time ago."

"What is it?"

"Dr. Smithson warned me not to get pregnant again for at least two years. If I did, there would be a chance I wouldn't carry it to term. We could lose another child."

Samuel let out a sigh. "Is this what's been bothering you for so long? Two years will go by quick, and I see no problem in waiting."

She dropped her head and whispered, "But Samuel, you don't understand. We can't share our marriage bed."

He lifted her chin up with his finger. "If the doctor said it would not be wise to conceive a child, so be it. I'm not worried about that, and neither should you be."

She twisted her eyes away from him. "But we can't use birth control."

Pulling her chin back in front of him he said, "We'll figure it out ...*together*."

Emma pulled the bible to her lap and ran her fingers through the pages until she found Ephesians. "I have to show you what *Mommi* shared with me."

When he saw her flip to Chapter 2, he placed his hands on the page and recited the verse. *"For by grace are ye saved through faith; and that not of yourselves: it is the gift of God: Not of works, lest any man should boast."*

Emma clasped his hand. "Ever since I got on the bus in Sugarcreek, the numbers two, eight, and nine have been showing up everywhere I turn."

He smiled and pulled her close. "Me too, but I tried to ignore their meaning. Instead, I looked for every opportunity to question your loyalty to me and let the devil play tricks in my head. He led me to believe you were sharing secrets with Alvin and your grandmother and put jealousy in my heart. It took Henry Mast to remind me to listen before I figured out what God was trying to tell me. I thought Henry was telling me to listen to you, but really, God used the old guy to remind me to listen to Him."

Samuel stood and helped Emma up. "It's time we both started listening to what He's trying to teach us. I'm certain He sent us to Pinecraft to prepare us for a battle much bigger than we can fight on our own."

"A battle?"

"*Jah.* He is preparing us to be His disciples, and that comes with a price. Once we learn what He has sent us here for, we won't be able to keep it to ourselves. Much like Alvin and Lynette, we'll have to share it. And that, my love, will cause friction at home, I'm sure of it."

Emma twisted the ribbon to her *kapp* between her fingers, "It already has?"

"How so?"

"Stella's letter. I mentioned it to my *datt,* and he was adamant I forget about it and keep it to myself."

"I'm sure he did. Have you told anyone else?"

"*Jah,* Katie."

"I'm not concerned with Katie."

"*Nee,* why?"

"Because Daniel believes the truth."

"He does?"

"Where do you think I got the bible? Why do you think he has so much trouble making it to church? He's already been questioned by the bishop more than once, and I'm confident they're second-guessing letting him join the church in the first place. Why do you think they try so hard to keep the English away? They don't want our young people to learn the truth. Daniel's been a threat from day one. If they weren't afraid of losing Katie to the English world, they might never have allowed them to marry."

Emma tucked her arm in the crook of his elbow. "What are we going to do?"

"To start with, we're going to church, and we may even stay to go to one of Alvin's bible studies. After that, I'm not sure, but we'll take it one day at a time and trust in the Lord and have faith he will pave our way."

Emma leaned her head on his shoulder. "I've missed you."

He smiled down at her. "I can't dispute that, but we had to go through all of this to get here."

CHAPTER 15

D aniel wore a path from the house to the barn. The brim of his hat was so snow-covered that he stopped to shake it off before entering the house. Katie, deep in the throes of labor, moaned a piercing cry that made him shudder.

"Are you sure there is nothing we can do to ease her pain?"

Ruth, Katie's mother, stood at the counter cutting slices of bread from a fresh loaf she'd brought over earlier. "Shouldn't be too much longer now. Maybe you should stay outside and tend to that mare about to foal. Strange as it is to have that mare birth in the winter; I think you're needed more outside. Besides, the midwife and I have everything under control in here."

Stomping the snow from his boots Daniel said. "I think I should stay, and besides, Levi is watching over the barn. I do wish Samuel was here. I could use his help right about now. Have you heard from him?"

Ruth brushed crumbs from the counter into her hand. "I checked the phone shanty early this afternoon, but still no word. I'm sure if Samuel hadn't found her, he would have called by now."

Daniel hung his coat on the back of the chair. "Katie was asking for Emma this morning. She knew her time was near and wanted her close by."

Ruth added jam to a slice of bread and handed it to Daniel. "They've always been so close. I'm sure she misses her."

Daniel licked a dollop of jam off the side of the bread but dropped it on the table when Katie's groan cut through the air. All color drained from his face as he looked at his mother-in-law when she exclaimed, "Trust me, you best go to the barn. I'll ring the bell when you should come back inside."

"Maybe you're right. I can't handle Katie in so much pain without being able to do anything about it."

Ruth giggled and wiped up the overturned bread from the table. "Not so sure watching your horse in labor will be any better, but it will keep your mind occupied."

Dusk added layers of gray to the snow-filled sky as Daniel made his way across the yard and back to the barn. Still void of life, Samuel and Emma's house sat as a cold reminder of the pain his best friend and sister endured. For days, he hid in the loft of the barn, praying and pleading with God to spare Katie and him the same sorrow. Snow collected on his short beard as he petitioned God one more time for a safe delivery for their new child.

Levi, Katie's father, had a headlamp secured to the brim of his hat and positioned it so the light illuminated the white and gray mare in the stall. Her labored breath danced in the filtered light.

"How's it going in there?" Levi asked.

"About the same as out here. I had to leave. Not sure how anyone can handle listening to that."

Levi lifted his foot and rested it on the rung of the gated fence. "When Samuel and Katie were born, I stayed far away from those birthing sounds. Too much for even a tough guy like me to handle."

Daniel let out a deep groan and shook his head. "And Katie thinks she wants a house full of *kinner*. I'm not too sure of that."

The mare rolled her head back, and they watched a contraction push the new foal's foot into view. "Much like in the house, all we can do is stand by and let nature take its course."

"*Jah*, but it's much easier watching a horse give birth than listening to my wife cry out in agony."

Levi lifted his chin. "God knew what he was doing when he put women in charge of childbearing. I don't think any of us could withstand labor, no matter how tough we were."

Heat rose from the freshly wet straw-covered floor as the mare continued to work through rolls of contractions, tightening her stomach. In a final push, the white sac covering the new foal came into view, and they both held their breath as its tiny head broke free.

"Amazing, isn't it? Just like that, new life makes its way into the world." Daniel nodded in agreement at the same time the dinner bell bounced off its cast-iron frame.

Levi lifted his chin in the direction of the house. "That's your call, go meet your new family. I'll stay here and make sure old Betsy takes to her new foal."

The walk back across the road took less than a few minutes, giving Daniel enough time to calm his racing pulse. Shedding his jacket and hat before he even opened the door, he threw them on the table while shuffling out of his boots.

A warm glow from the upstairs oil lamp seeped down the stairs, and Ruth waved him up with a smile. "All is well."

Relief outlined Daniel's jaw as he took the stairs two at a time. When he stepped into their room, Katie's face was flushed, and wisps of dark hair were painted on her forehead with moisture. Her voice cracked. "Come meet your daughter."

"A girl? We have a daughter?"

Daniel sat on the side of the bed and kissed Katie on the forehead. "Are you okay?"

"Better than okay, look at her. Isn't she beautiful?"

"Are you sure she's okay?"

"Yes, we're both perfect."

He let out a long sigh and ran his fingers through his hair. "I was so worried."

Katie tilted her chin in his direction. "Didn't you have faith God would protect us?'

"No, it wasn't that at all ...it was ...well you know ...everything Emma went through and all."

"You can breathe now. I'm good, and so is Elizabeth."

"Elizabeth?"

Katie looked up at Daniel. "What do you think?"

"You want to name her after Emma's birth name?"

"I want to clear it with Emma and Samuel first, but I can't think of any other name that suits her better."

Daniel touched his daughter's dark downy hair. "It might mean we can't officially name her until they return home. I'm not sure when that might be. Can you wait?"

"I can and will. Emma is like a *schwester* to me, and I can't think of any other name that would suit us either."

"But what if she comes back, but she still doesn't want to have anything to do with us?"

"Oh Daniel, that won't happen. She just went through a rough spot. When she lays eyes on Elizabeth and holds her in her arms, all will be well, I'm certain of it."

Daniel squeezed his wife's hand. "This is the best Christmas present ever."

***

After over twenty hours on the bus, Samuel and Emma stepped off. They leaned into one another to block the wind whipping around the bus terminal in Pittsburgh. Samuel arranged for a driver to pick them up and even agreed to the increased fair since it was the first of January.

"Samuel, maybe we should have stayed in Florida until winter broke. I say we turn around and hop back on a bus going south."

Samuel wrapped his arm around her shoulder. "We'll go back, but right now, we need to start this new year with a fresh start."

"My stomach is churning."

Samuel gulped a lungful of frosty air, "Are you ill?"

"No, nothing like that," Emma placed her hand over her stomach, "I'm nervous."

They headed toward their driver's familiar sedan, and Samuel added, "We need to separate what we feel from the One we serve."

They both placed their bags in the open trunk. "You're right, but I'm still scared."

Samuel opened her door and waited until she slid across the backseat. "And rightly so. God never told us being one of his disciples would be easy."

Emma rubbed her hands together. "*Jah*, I suppose not."

Samuel and Emma stayed quiet in the hour it took to get from the bus depot to their home in Willow Springs. Both lost in their own thoughts about what the future might bring. Since Christmas, Alvin and Lynette had spent almost every day sharing different passages and stories from the bible to help them understand what God wanted them to see. So much truth had been kept from them, and they now felt it was their mission to spread the Word. How or when that might happen was still a mystery, but they agreed they would take one day at a time and wait for God to pave their way.

Snow gathered on the front porch of the *doddi haus,* and Samuel held Emma's arm tightly while she made it up the stairs. "Perhaps tomorrow we can start moving into the new house, *jah?*"

Emma pushed open the door and stomped her feet before stepping inside. "I'd like that, for sure and certain."

Emma snickered when she saw the sink filled with dirty dishes. "My punishment for leaving you alone for two weeks."

"Sorry about that; I meant to take care of those."

She slipped out of her jacket and kissed her husband's cheek. "Give me a few minutes, and I'll fix us some dinner.

Maybe after that, we can go visit with Daniel and Katie. I have some apologies to make."

It was good to have his Emma back. He didn't want to do anything but keep her to himself all evening. But he knew their family missed them, and they would be anxious to see them both. Emma stood in front of the calendar to flip it to the New Year, brought her hand to her mouth, and gasped, "Katie will have had her baby by now."

Samuel's voice, filled with concern, asked, "Would you rather not go over?"

Emma stammered, "It will be hard, I'm sure, and I pray she'll forgive me for my unacceptable behavior."

Samuel smiled tenderly at his wife. "I know my *schwester,* and that's the last thing you need to worry about."

"Can dinner wait? I'd really like to go see them now."

Samuel held out her coat, and she slipped her arms back in the still warm lining. "As long as you keep that smile on your face, my stomach can wait as long as you need."

***

Katie sat in a rocker near the front window and watched a dark car pull into her parent's driveway. Curious as to why her parents would call for a driver on New Year's Day, she tucked Elizabeth in the crook of her arm and moved to the kitchen window. From her view across Mystic Mill Road, she watched as her best friend stepped out of the car. The tenderness of the way her *bruder* helped her up the stairs revealed so much more than words could say.

"Daniel, come quick."

Daniel ran up the stairs from the basement and breathlessly asked, "What is it? What do you need?"

'Look, Emma's back."

"Well, I'll be."

"Hurry, put your boots on and go ask them to come to visit."

"Now Katie, are you sure? How about we let them settle first. They'll come to see us when they're ready. And besides, I don't think you or the *baby* need any excitement yet."

"No, please, I want Emma to meet her."

Daniel took Katie's elbow and guided her back to the living room. "Let's see how Emma's state of mind is first. Perhaps it's too soon for her to see our child."

Katie's bluebird eyes fluttered in hopes she could change his mind. "I'm certain she's better. I can feel it."

"Now, don't go batting those eyelashes at me; you know I can't say no to you when you do that."

Katie blushed. "Please, Daniel, go ask them to come over." He mumbled as he headed to the boot rack. "If she says one word to upset you, I'll send her home."

"Quit, she won't, I'm sure of it."

No sooner did Daniel get his boots on than Samuel knocked on the back door.

Surprised at their guests, Daniel stepped back and waved them in. "I was just heading your way. Katie was adamant you come to visit."

Emma removed her coat. "The baby?"

"Yep, she was born on Christmas Eve."

Emma put both hands over her heart. "A girl?"

"*Jah*, go see for yourself. Katie's dying for you to meet her."

Emma moved closer to her brother. "Please forgive me for the way I treated you both. It was uncalled for, and I'm so sorry."

Daniel pulled her into a big bear hug. "You have nothing to worry about here; all is good."

Emma pushed through the lump forming in the back of her throat and whispered, "*Denki*."

"Now go meet your niece," Daniel pointed to the front room.

Samuel followed close on Emma's heels and stopped a few feet from where his *schwester* sat in the rocker. "You can come closer, Samuel." Katie shifted and turned the baby's face in their direction.

Emma held her hands out. "May I?"

The room seemed warm, and Emma was cautious not to lose her footing in her dream-like state. Everything around her faded away as she picked up the tightly wrapped bundle from Katie's arms. She backed up toward the twin rocker to Katie's left and kissed the child's forehead. "Well, hello there, Miss..." she looked toward Katie, "What did you name her?"

"That's just it. We wanted to wait until you got back to officially reveal her name."

"Why? It doesn't matter to me what you call her."

Katie patted Emma's knee. "But it does because we couldn't think of a better fitting name than Elizabeth."

Emma's chest tightened. "You want to give her my biological birth name?"

Unsure of Emma's response, Katie asked, "Would you mind?"

"Heaven's no, unless Samuel has any objection."

Both women looked Samuel's way. "None from me."

"Wonderful, then Elizabeth it is." Emma ran her fingers along the side of the baby girl's face. "Hello there, Elizabeth, I'm your Aunt Emma." The baby cooed and stretched out her hand until it touched Emma's chin. Emma took her tiny fingers and kissed them as they gripped her thumb. For the first time in months, Emma felt true joy. Holding her niece set a longing in her heart. But at that moment, sharing in the beauty of new life with her best friend didn't compare to anything else she'd ever experienced.

Daniel elbowed Samuel. "Want to see what I'm working on downstairs?"

Samuel looked in Emma's direction. "You good?"

"Better than good, I'm perfect. Go, do whatever you two do in the basement. Katie and I have some catching up to do."

After the men's heavy footsteps faded, Katie leaned into Emma and asked, "How are you?"

Emma replied, "Better, not great but better." Without looking up from Elizabeth's face.

"Daniel said you went to Florida. Is that true?"

"*Jah*, I went to Pinecraft. I stayed with my *Mommi* Shetler and her *schwester*.

Katie's eyebrows raised. "Your biological father's mother? How was that?"

"It was good. *Mommi* Lillian helped me work through some things."

A comforting hush filled the room while both women found their footing in their life-long friendship. "Katie, can you forgive me for being so ugly with you?"

"You have already been forgiven, and we don't need to speak of it again."

Emma pulled Elizabeth's tiny fingers to her lips. She whispered, "It was easier for me to allow myself to be consumed by my grief. But I finally had to face the fact that God had bigger plans."

Katie asked in a wistful tone. "So you're not mad at God anymore?"

"I'm not saying I understand all of what he has in store, but I'm better equipped to accept it now. If nothing else, losing James made me aware of my own mortality."

Confused, Katie asked, "How so?"

"Let's just say I figured out I could spend my life mourning over what I lost, or I could find ways to rejoice at what I've gained. In this case, I choose the latter. And sometimes I have to find that joy multiple times throughout the day."

"I'm proud of you Emma. I can't imagine what I'd feel like if we lost Elizabeth, but I'll thank the Lord for every day we have with her."

The baby started to fuss, and Emma handed her back to Katie. "Part of me didn't understand the array of emotions I was dealing with, and I blamed both God and Samuel. It was easier to distance myself from you and my family rather than face the exhausting reality."

Katie waited until Elizabeth latched onto her swollen bosom before answering, "I'm sorry I didn't insist you let me help you through all of that."

"There is no need to have any regret. I don't think I was in any state of mind to graciously accept even if you offered."

Katie pulled a blanket over the baby's head. "I'm sure the Lord has a reason for everything He put you through."

Emma crossed her legs and lifted her heel from the floor to set her chair in motion. "You'll never comprehend how God will use you until you let Him."

Katie took a sip from a drink on her stand before asking, "Do you have any idea what He has planned?"

"A lot of things were revealed to Samuel and me when we were in Florida. We met a young couple who lost a child as well, and they were wonderful in helping us see through losing James."

"Oh, how wonderful. I can sympathize with you, but to truly understand your pain, I just couldn't, no matter how hard I tried."

"I understand, really I do. Lynette showed me that God hears when we cry out to him and if He has to tell us no, it's for our protection." Emma paused long enough to decide whether she wanted to share her next thought with the one person, other than Samuel she trusted with her life.

"Protection? What would He be protecting you from?"

"Maybe protecting isn't the right word, but He wants us to grow...*grow in Christ*."

Katie shook her head. "Must be mommy brain kicking in, but I really don't understand what you're trying to say."

Emma moved toward the kitchen. "It doesn't matter right now. How about I fix dinner? I bet you have more in your refrigerator than I do. Things are pretty slim at my house."

"That would be wonderful. There's a slew of casseroles in there and way too much food for just Daniel and me."

Making herself at home in Katie's kitchen, Emma worked on getting a meal on the table. Her heart swelled at wanting to share everything she and Samuel learned in Pinecraft, but Alvin's warning about taking it slow weighed on her mind. Katie took her baptism vows seriously, and it would take more than a few words to show her the true meaning of salvation through Christ. The excitement that kept building in her chest about sharing the truth with those she loved mingled deep in her stomach, making it hard to concentrate on anything else.

***

Daniel pulled an extra stool up to the workbench in the basement and nodded his head for Samuel to take a seat.

"So good to see Emma smile."

"*Jah*, Florida was good for her."

"And you?"

"I'm good."

"Are you sure about that?"

Samuel pushed the towel away from the bible Daniel kept hidden in the basement. "Emma's been reading."

"An English bible?"

"*Jah*."

"Have you told her about us studying together?"

"*Jah*."

Daniel picked up a chisel and started to smooth out a piece of wood. "Do you think she'll tell Katie?"

"It's not her place."

Daniel brushed wood chips into the bin under the bench, "True."

"You'll need to tell her sooner than later."

"Katie won't be as open as we are about going against the *Ordnung.*"

"Daniel, Bishop Weaver is already questioning you about your motives for joining the Amish church. As soon as he gets word of us attending a bible study, he'll certainly blame you."

"But I didn't tell you to do that."

"No, you didn't, but I can bet the Amish grapevine will make its way up here from Pinecraft before too long. We didn't hide spending almost every day with Alvin and Lynette Miller for the last week. It's sure to make its way back to Willow Springs. I even met old man Mast's *bruder*."

"That's not good. Who are the Millers?"

"A Mennonite couple who ministers to young people. They say their mission in life is to convert Old Order teens into discovering the truth of Jesus. Lynette got a hold of Emma, and ... well, you know the rest of the story."

"So that explains Emma's change."

"I can't take any credit for that. In fact, I made things pretty difficult the first few days I was there."

Daniel shook his head. "This isn't going to go well for any of us, is it?"

"You're not telling me anything I don't already know. I just hope we can keep it to ourselves for a while until I figure out what to do."

"Don't think you have to carry that weight yourself. I was the one who brought it to your attention in the first place."

"I didn't have to read it. That was my choice."

Daniel picked up a piece of sandpaper and ran it the length of the wood in his hands. "Let me figure out how I'm going to tell Katie first, then we can go from there."

"We can't turn back now. Emma and I have already made up our minds about it. If it comes between serving God or adhering to the *Ordnung*, we will choose God."

"As you should."

"I had some intense conversations with Alvin while in Pinecraft. He helped me see my first responsibility is to God and then my family. Knowing what I know now, how can I raise my family in believing the only way to get to heaven is by following a set of rules and guidelines someone other than God dictates to us?"

Daniel stopped sanding long enough to say. "Exactly what I've been struggling with for the past two years."

Samuel opened the bible and started to fan through the pages. "It will get worse. I feel it. Now that Emma and I know the truth, how can we follow anything else?"

"You can't."

Samuel closed the book, "I'm not sure how you've gone on all this time sidestepping the truth when it's right here in black and white."

"At the time, I didn't think it would be so much of an issue. I've never told Katie what I truly believe. If I did, she might not have married me."

"Man, you can't keep something like this from her. You have to tell her before Bishop Weaver pays us all a visit."

"*Jah*, I know you're right, but man, I hope we can hold off for a few weeks. She just had Elizabeth last week."

CHAPTER 16

Somewhere in the wee hours of the morning, Emma rolled over and wrapped her arm around Samuel's middle. Not realizing he was awake, she snuggled into the curve of his spine just as he brought her hand to his lips. Without saying a word, he rolled to his back and tucked his arm under her head and kissed her forehead. The rooster was already making morning known even before the first rays of light filtered through the blue pleated curtains. For so long, she denied the warmth of his love. She took advantage of every ounce of the day to be in his embrace. His strong arms squeezed her tight one last time before he rolled out of bed.

She rubbed a circle in the warm spot. "So soon?"

His raspy voice said more than just a few words. "I best put distance between us."

There was no denying what he meant, and she felt him pull away from their closeness more than once over the last couple of weeks. She folded her arm under her head and wiped away a tear from her cheek. There had to be another way; she couldn't imagine turning him away for two years.

After his bare feet made it down their newly sanded stairs, she pushed aside the covers and dressed. They'd spent the last few days moving out of the *doddi haus* and into their new one, and it would be the first day she could put some routine back in her life. Samuel, Levi, and Daniel were getting back to building a bigger counter at the bakery, and she ...well ...she wasn't quite sure what she'd do. Perhaps she'd visit with her *datt* and *schwesters*, or better yet, she'd see if she could see Dr. Smithson. The smell of coffee floated up the stairs, and she followed it to the kitchen.

She pulled the curtain above the sink to the side and asked, "I need to go to town, and I thought I'd visit my *datt*."

"Not a problem, I'll hitch Oliver up for you. What do you need in town?"

She continued to stare out the window, hoping to find the right words so as not to alarm him. "I ...I want to see Dr. Smithson."

Samuel stopped his cup in midair. "Why? Is something wrong?"

"No, not exactly."

"Then what is it?"

"I didn't ask him enough questions last time, and I want to see what our options might be."

"Options for what?"

She walked over and pulled out a chair at the table beside him. "You know ...our ...*options*."

His upper lip turned to a thin line. "We know what our options are; there's no reason why we have to look for others."

She laid her hand across his forearm. "Marie said we had other choices. I have to learn what they might be."

"If it's anything we have to go to the bishop about, I'd just as soon stay under his radar."

"Why? Has he already come to call on you?"

"No, not yet, but let's keep it that way."

"Let me go talk to Dr. Smithson. I can't believe I'm the first Amish woman who needed other alternatives to prevent pregnancy."

"But you know as well as I do; we are to put these things in God's hand."

"Samuel, we can't put another child in harm's way. We must listen to Dr. Smithson's advice. Besides, if we're going to upturn the apple cart around here, we'll be in no position to bring a child into that. When word gets out about us being re-baptized in Florida, it won't only be the bishop who calls on us. We can count on that."

"I suppose no one will think twice about you going to see the doctor again. But just remember I won't be going to clear anything with the bishop."

She stood and pushed her chair in. "Let me see what he has to say first. There may not be anything we can do, but I have to find out for sure first."

Their chocolate lab, Someday, started to bark at the front door a few seconds before a knock announced an arrival. Emma patted the dog on its head before opening it to see who stood on the porch. "*Datt,* what a nice surprise. I was planning to stop by today."

He kicked the toe of each boot on the door frame before he stepped inside. "Levi stopped by yesterday and said you made it back."

"*Jah*, we did. We've spent the last couple of days moving in." She kissed his cheek before saying, "Come see how nice the cupboards you made us look. I just love them."

"I can't stay long. I have a couple of orders I need to finish, but I have a matter I want to discuss with you."

"Okay, come sit down. Can I get you anything? A cup of coffee or cocoa?"

"*Nee*, really, I can't stay."

"What is it, *datt*?"

Her father looked at her and then to Samuel, "I want to see the letter your *mamm* left you."

Emma moved to the drawer near the sink, "The one she left with the shawl?"

"*Jah*, that's the one."

She handed her father the pink envelope, and he looked to Samuel and asked, "Have you read this?"

"*Jah*."

His stern voice spoke in not much more than a whisper, "You both need to forget it ever existed." Before Emma could protest, her father walked to the sink, took a lighter from his pocket, and set it on fire.

Emma ran to his side and tried to grab it from his hands. He twisted away and watched it wither away in flames. "*Datt*, what are you doing!"

"No good will come from this, and it will only cause separation."

"But *Datt*, that was my letter, not yours! *Mamm* left it for me, not you."

"And she did so against my wishes."

Samuel moved to his wife's side. "I mean no disrespect Jacob, but that was uncalled for. If Stella's last dying wish was for Emma to find out the truth about Jesus, what right do you have to take that away from her?"

Emma squeezed Samuel's hand. "It doesn't matter now. I have her words etched right here." She laid her hand over her heart. "I don't need a piece of paper to remind me what she wanted to teach me."

Her father picked his hat up from the table and said, "While my job with you has long been completed, I have to leave your fate in your husband's hands. However, I warn you if I hear you've shared this with your *schwesters,* you won't have to worry about being excommunicated. I'll do that myself."

Emma lowered her head and tried to appeal to her father's softer side. "You can't be serious?"

"When it comes to matters like this, I am. You both have made promises before God and the church. To go back on them now will force my hand in more ways than one. You realize what it would mean if you pursued this, don't you?"

Samuel stiffened his shoulders and stood face to face with Jacob. "Emma is my concern now, and I'll deal with this in my own way."

Jacob didn't move his eyes from Samuel's face. "Just as my household is my concern. Even though Rebecca and Anna are older than Emma by three years, they still live under my roof, which means they fall under my care."

He turned to face Emma. "You will not be permitted to see your *schwesters* or me if you share this with them."

Jacob let himself out and they didn't breathe until his footsteps left the porch. Emma turned and let Samuel pull her into a hug. "We can't promise him we won't speak the truth, can we?"

"*Nee*, my love, we can't. If Rebecca and Anna want to learn the truth, God will make it possible with or without us."

She looked up and found his eyes. "It will happen, I'm sure of it."

"How can you be so sure?"

"Because *Mamm* left the same letter for both of them as well. In due time they will go through something in their lives that Ruth will be called on to hand them a gift, much like she handed me mine."

Samuel ran his finger along her jawline. "Then you see, my love, it is already out of our hands."

Emma buried her head in his chest. "It's starting already, isn't it?"

"*Jah*, we're being called into battle in the name of Jesus Christ."

***

Levi started a fire in the woodstove that sat in the bakery corner long before Samuel and Daniel showed up to help. In three short months, the girls would need to open back up Yoder's Bakery. For the past two years, they'd only opened from March until October. But starting soon, they would be opened year-round. A much bigger counter and the addition of seating meant the community could enjoy fresh pies and cookies whenever they wanted.

The front door sprung opened, and he waved the bishop in. "Bishop Weaver, what do I owe this visit to?"

"Good morning, Levi. I see you are making headway with opening the bakery soon." The old man patted his stomach. "I know for sure I'll be making it one of my favorite stops again."

"*Jah*, you and me both."

Bishop Weaver pulled over a paint bucket and took a seat. He pointed to another. "Join me."

Levi straddled the other bucket and took a red shop rag out of his back pocket to wipe paint from his hands. "Something on your mind?"

The bishop rested his folded arms across his belly. "You know we are down two ministers. Abe Stutzman moved to Byler's District, and Harvey Hershberger is on his way to his forever home."

Levi's shoulders slumped. "Don't tell me you feel my name may be added to the list of nominees to fill one of those spots."

"It very well may be. Both you and Jacob Byler are well-respected members of our church, and I have all faith the congregation will nominate you both once again."

"Jacob? Have you told him yet?"

"I stopped by and talked with Jacob and his new wife early this morning. I reminded him as I am reminding you the responsibility that comes with such a calling. We won't know for sure until Sunday who the community chooses, but in the end, God will have the final say."

Levi was at a loss for words. There was no other time in an Amish man's life that was so disturbing than to hear he was to be called into a life of service. The responsibility didn't come lightly, and most times, it came with a heavy burden. He'd seen it more than once. When a man's Lot was chosen, you often heard his wife cry in agony. Life as they'd known it ...was gone ...*forever*.

Bishop Weaver stood and extended his hand. "May God's calling be upon you, and may you accept it in service to the Lord."

Levi stood and shook the man's hand even though his insides were burdensome. Not for himself, but for Ruth and his family. If his name was called, his family would be under strict scrutiny. Everything they did would be watched, and they would be expected to uphold every ounce of the *Ordnung*, with no exceptions.

274

There would be no doubt about it. Levi would have to pull his family together that evening and explain what being called into ministry would mean to them all. His concern wasn't with Samuel, Katie, or even Emma, but he worried about Daniel. The boy had been raised English, and it would fall much harder on his ears than anyone else. He already had his doubts about him following their strict conservative order. But he knew Daniel loved his daughter Katie, so he was sure he would comply.

***

Emma tied a blue scarf over her *kapp* and picked up two plates of pie. "I'm going to take dessert out to Samuel and Daniel. I'll be back in a few minutes."

Katie was busy changing Elizabeth's diaper in the front room. She hollered toward the kitchen. "I'm sure they'll be back in a few minutes. They said they wanted to just check on the new foal."

"I don't mind; I'll be right back." Emma hurried out the door before Katie could protest again. After Levi's announcement after supper, she knew exactly why her husband and *bruder* retreated to the barn before dessert. Thank goodness Ruth had a headache and left as soon as supper was over. She needed to talk to Daniel and Samuel. She balanced the two plates in one hand and pushed the heavy barn door aside. Light filtered in the tack room, and she followed the glow. Standing in the doorway, she waited until both men turned her way. "This is horrible news, isn't it?"

Samuel was the first to speak. "Regardless, there are two spots. One or both of our fathers may soon be ministers."

She handed them each a dish and took forks from her pocket. "This has to be why my *datt* was so adamant this morning."

Daniel picked up a bite of pie but stopped to ask, "What happened?"

Samuel spoke up. "He made sure we both knew we were to bury Stella's letter and never bring it up to anyone. He so much as already told us he would excommunicate us, regardless of if we were family or not."

Emma leaned on the workbench. "He's worried I might say something to Rebecca or Anna."

Daniel propped his foot on the wall and leaned back as he finished his pie. Scooping the last bite in his mouth, he set the plate on the bench. "I haven't found the right time to tell Katie yet."

"Tell me what?"

Emma stood up straight, and Samuel moved aside, so she could come into the tack room with them.

"Daniel, what do you need to tell me, and why does everyone know but me?"

Daniel reached out and took her hand. "We can talk about it later."

Snapping away from his grasp. "No, we can talk about it now. If there is something the three of you are keeping from me, I want to know it now."

Emma walked to her. "Come on, Katie, let's go check on Elizabeth. Daniel can explain it to you after we leave."

Her voice squeaked, "No, now."

Emma pulled her shoulders up and looked at Daniel. "She needs to know; it affects us all."

Samuel pulled out a stool and patted its seat. Daniel cleared his throat and buried his hands deep in his pockets. "Samuel and Emma have been studying the bible."

"Why would that be a big secret?"

Daniel pushed a clump of straw around on the floor with the toe of his boot. "I gave Samuel an English bible."

Katie covered her ears with both hands. "No, I can't hear this."

Daniel pulled her hands away and looked her in the eye. "Katie, I've been reading it as well."

Katie moaned, "Whhyyy?"

"Because I've been questioning the *Ordnung* and what it stands for. I don't believe my only way to heaven is how well I follow a set of rules. God tells us the only way we can make it to heaven is through Jesus."

She grabbed his hands and held on tight as he cupped her face and she asked, "How on earth can we get to heaven through Jesus? This isn't right. We made a promise, we can't go back on our word."

Samuel stated, "We can, and we must."

She pulled his hand away and looked to Emma. "Please, talk some sense into them. We can't read any bible, but our High German one. We promised."

Emma came and knelt in front of her best friend. "But Katie, we don't understand that one. I learned we can be rest assured of our salvation through Christ. There is no other way to the Lord but through Jesus. Samuel and I both have been re-baptized as Amish Christians."

"What do you mean re-baptized?"

"Our friends Alvin and Lynette opened a whole new world to us. One where we don't even have to guess if we'll make it to heaven. Don't you want the same thing?"

Katie wiped her nose on her coat sleeve. "Daniel, how could you?"

"I tried to keep it from you for as long as I could. But it's the truth, and you have to know it as well. I want us to rely on God's Word, not on a set of rules."

"That's just it. You shouldn't have kept it from me at all. How long have you doubted your vows?"

Daniel tried to reach out, but she pulled away. "Did you feel this way on our wedding day?"

"*Jah.*"

"Then why did you marry me and agree to raise our family in the ways of our Old Order community?"

"Because I love you."

"You lied to me, ...to God ...and to our family!"

"I didn't lie to God. He knew my heart."

"A lie is a sin, Daniel, don't try to play it off that one is any less offensive than another."

"Katie, please listen to me. I didn't plan any of this. I had no idea Emma was going to figure out the truth. I didn't tell her or convince her to believe anything."

Emma took Katie's hand. "He didn't. This was all my doing. Samuel didn't even tell me he and Daniel had been studying the bible together until a couple of weeks ago."

"You poisoned my *bruder* against the church too?"

Samuel declared, "He did no such thing, and he didn't twist my arm. I did it all on my own. All we did together was talk about what we read."

Katie turned, threw her arms up in the air. "We'll be put in the *bann* for sure."

CHAPTER 17

Sunday morning brought an onslaught of unseasonably warm weather. A bright January sun glistened through the trees as Samuel guided Oliver to fall into step behind Levi and Daniel's buggies. The slow and steady procession gave them all plenty of time to contemplate how the Lot would fall. The process of opening one of the three books that soon would be set in front of Jacob, Levi, and Henry Schrock added a heaviness to the day. Each man would put their fate in the hands of the Lord and respectively would accept the outcome without complaint.

Earlier, Emma noticed Ruth held tightly to a handkerchief as she crawled inside Levi's buggy. If they only knew the secret they shared with Daniel and Katie, her tears would be much harder to control.

The landscape was dotted with brown-topped buggies as they made their way to Bishop Weaver's farm on the outskirts of Willow Springs. Samuel reached over and squeezed Emma's gloved hand. "What are you so deep in thought about?"

Emma took her other hand and laid it over her husband's. "I'm a little anxious about what this will do to my *datt*. He already suspects we have questions. If he is one of the chosen, it may add a deeper wedge between us. How can he accept his calling knowing his daughter and son-in-law may challenge his position?"

"Emma, I'm not going to worry about today or what might happen. The best thing we can do is keep what we are learning to ourselves for now. God will show us when the time is right to share what we know. Just like Alvin and Lynette were put in our path, He will line other people up with us when the time is right."

"What about Katie? She's so upset with Daniel. I already sense strife between them." Emma said.

"Again, we can't fret about that. Daniel will lead her and Elizabeth in his own manner. I know my *schwester*, she'll come around, just give her time. All we can do is pray for them and get out of God's way. He'll do the rest."

Emma nodded, "You're right." She leaned in and nudged his shoulder. "How did you get so smart about things like this?"

He grinned and elbowed her. "You see ...I've been reading this book that's teaching me such things."

She wrapped her arm around his and hugged it tightly. "I love our evening studies. But more than that, I enjoy hearing how you interpret God's word."

He snuggled close without taking his eyes off the road or letting up on the reins. "God is preparing us. I can feel it."

"How can you be sure?"

Samuel paused a few seconds before responding. "It's like a burning feeling way down deep in my belly. An ache that won't go away until I tell someone. But the thing is, I don't want it to go away. I want it to grow bigger and better. Does that make sense?"

Emma gave it some thought. "It does because I feel the same way. It really started the day we went to the ocean, so Alvin could re-baptize us. When I came up out of the water, something happened inside of me. It was like the bright sun could finally reach the spot in my heart covered in the shade. I felt like one of my sunflowers that turn their face to the sun all summer long. I want that warm feeling every day of my life."

Emma got quiet for a few minutes and then added, "I hope Katie will experience that someday too."

Samuel snapped his tongue at Oliver. "She will, I'm sure of it. We just need to give God time to work on her heart, much like he did ours."

***

Katie held on tightly to Elizabeth when the buggy shifted, forcing her to slide closer to Daniel. "Sorry."

"There is no need to say sorry. I like my girls sitting close."

Katie took a hand and pushed herself closer to the canvas door. The air was thick inside the enclosed buggy, and Katie wished they could find a way to fix what was between them. No matter how many times they tried to discuss the issue, she couldn't get past how betrayed she felt. He had turned into something Katie was afraid to embrace. What he was asking her to believe was so far from what she'd been taught that she saw no outcome but complete isolation from her family and friends.

When Daniel left late last night, she watched as he walked across the road and onto Samuel and Emma's porch. There was no doubt in her mind they had a plan to study the bible together.

He didn't ask her if she wanted to join them. Instead, he slipped out of bed after he assumed she was asleep. The treachery of their secret meeting etched a deep void in her heart.

She stole a glance his way as he concentrated on the slushy road. There was no doubt she was in love with him, but what he was doing would cause heartache at some point. How could he go against her and what they stood for? A sudden glimpse of life without him flashed before her eyes. Would he walk away from her and Elizabeth to follow the ways of his English background? In the Amish world, divorce was not an option. But Daniel was not Amish. He was just an English man in Amish clothing. Would she or Elizabeth be enough to hold on to him, or would she have to give up everything she held so dear to be with him? If only she knew what to do. A small gasp escaped her lips, and she swallowed hard to stop tears from taking hold.

"What is it, Katie? Something is bothering you this morning."

She turned her head away from his stare. "Nothing I can't figure out on my own."

"But you don't need to figure things out on your own; I'm here to help."

Katie focused her eyes on the road. "Really? How can you say we figure things out together? You didn't come to me when you decided to slip out of bed last night and turn to Samuel and Emma instead of me."

Daniel stiffened his shoulders. "In all fairness, you've not been very receptive to what we want to share with you."

"I'm not and never will be. You chose to explore these things behind my back. That was your decision, not mine. So don't tell me we figure things out together."

Her hands shook when she tucked the blanket around Elizabeth. She never raised her voice to Daniel before, and Elizabeth squirmed with her tone. He didn't utter a word in response to her outburst but kept his eyes fixated on her father's buggy in front of them.

***

Ruth twisted the thin white layer of linen in her hands. "My heart is full this morning."

Levi patted his wife's knee. "Mine too, my love, but we'll thank the Lord for whatever he puts in front of us today, agreed?"

"Agreed, and I have faith you'll be ready for whatever He asks of you, even if it means life as we know it, will be no more."

Levi tried to lighten the mood by adding, "Now, now, Ruth, it won't be that bad. I might have to give up our Saturday night Scrabble game, but besides that, I can't see things changing much."

Ruth gave him a nervous smile before asking, "Who are you trying to convince, you or me?"

"A little of both. We have to remember God makes no mistakes, and He is already aware of the outcome of today's Lot assignment."

Ruth turned to glance over her shoulder. "I'm worried about Katie. Something's off, but I can't pinpoint it. I think maybe she has some post-baby blues."

"I haven't noticed, but again I've been preoccupied the last few days. Maybe Katie just needs a long visit from her *mamm*."

"Maybe so, I'll walk over this afternoon and see if I can take care of Elizabeth, so she can take a nap or something."

Levi pulled back on the reins to slow his horse to turn into Bishop Weaver's long driveway. "Here goes. Are you ready?"

Ruth sucked in a long breath. "Is it wrong I've been praying someone else's name will be on the list today other than yours?"

"If it is, then I'm just as guilty."

"The Lord is with us all," Ruth added as they came to a stop in front of the procession, making their way to Bishop Weaver's white farmhouse.

***

Emma and Katie fell into step behind the line of women making their way into the kitchen. Bishop Weaver's wife stood at the back door, welcoming each inside with a holy kiss and a warm smile. As Emma made her way to the women's side, she noted three empty chairs placed at the front of the room. A small table sat off to the side with three *Ausbund* songbooks neatly tied closed with a string. Two of the black leather hymnals contained a small slip of paper with a scripture written on it. Whichever man chose the book with the bible verse inside would commit his life into service to the Lord.

She let Katie step in front of her when she stopped to ponder over what it might mean if her father was one of the chosen. Rebecca, her older *schwester,* gave her a slight shove to take her seat beside Katie and Elizabeth. There was a coldness in Katie's greeting that she half expected. Once again, Emma found herself at odds with her best friend, but the coolness came from Katie this time. She had to find a way to clear the air between them. Perhaps she'd go visit with her that afternoon. All they needed to do was talk it out, and all would be well again. She was sure of it.

Rebecca leaned in and muttered in Emma's ear. "*Datt* seemed nervous this morning. I'm not sure why. If his name gets added to the Lot today, it's what God had in store for his life, and he needs to just accept it." The tone of her older *schwester's* voice always grated on Emma's nerves. No matter what it was, Rebecca had a way of using the nip in her voice to emphasize the negative of a situation.

Emma hushed her and replied, "Did you ever stop to think he may feel the pressure of what being a minister would mean to all of us?"

Rebecca wouldn't be quieted and added, "We don't have anything to hide. I think him being chosen would be an honor to our family. Don't you?"

Again, Emma tried to quiet Rebecca and replied through gritted teeth, "Do you need to speak so loudly?"

Rebecca sat up straight and opened the *Ausbund* to the first song, "But don't you think he would be respected by the community if he was a minister? And besides, he should have been chosen the last time."

"Rebecca, you know as well as I do it would be prideful to think that way. *Datt* isn't like that. He's a humble man and will want to uphold the guidelines of our community just like his ancestors did before him. He will take the job seriously and won't act like nobility, I'm certain of it."

Rebecca turned away from Emma in defiance at her rebuttal. "Oh, that's right, all-mighty Emma has all the answers like always."

Emma said a silent prayer that God would change Rebecca's prideful heart, and he'd make her and Samuel's path clear. Her heart ached with the thought it might come down to her father's charge to excommunicate them if their secret was ever revealed.

Nearly three hours later, after the last minister spoke, Bishop Weaver stood and directed his comments to the whole congregation. "God instructs all men to be in good standing with the church to accept the Lot. Before I read the names of those nominated, let me remind you that each of these men is known to be filled with faith, exhibit blameless self-control, and are good managers of their household. At the time of the adult baptism, each man here agreed to uphold the position of minister, if he should be called."

The entire congregation followed Bishop Weaver's lead and dropped to their knees. Each member silently prayed for the men whose names would soon be revealed. When the bishop cleared his throat, each person quietly slipped back on their bench and waited.

The communion service fell way into the afternoon as each man held his breath, praying his name would not fall from their bishop's lips. "As I call each name, please walk to the front of the room. Retrieve a book from the table and take a seat in one of the chairs in front of me."

Not a single sound was heard, not even a whimper from a hungry toddler or restless infant. It was as if they knew God's hand would fall among them.

Without so much as an introduction, the bishop read the names before him; "Henry Schrock, ...Levi Yoder, and ...Jacob Byler."

Emma looked across the room to Samuel and Daniel. Samuel's face fell an ashen gray, and Daniel's followed suit.

Rebecca reached over and tapped Emma's knee as if she was waiting for her own name to be called. While everyone else in the room felt the burden for the three men, it was as if Rebecca found pleasure in her father's nomination. Emma twisted her leg away from her *schwester's* touch and turned toward Katie just in time to see her wipe moisture from her cheek. Katie felt it too. Soon one of their fathers would be called into service, and its heaviness hit them both.

Like in slow motion, Emma watched her father walk to the table and pick up one of the books. As he turned to look out over the congregation, he locked his eyes on her. Somewhere deep behind his dark lashes, her father pleaded with her without saying a word. When he turned to take a chair, her heart picked up its rhythm, and tears began to build behind her eyes.

After the three men had selected a book, Bishop Weaver moved in front of Henry Schrock. Holding his hand out, he took the book, pulled the string, and searched for a single slip of paper. When his fingers stopped where the page was marked, he pulled the paper and handed it back to Henry. In the seat right in front of Emma, Maggie Schrock inhaled and dropped her head. It was evident to everyone around her that she felt the responsibility her husband was just handed. Next, the bishop moved to Levi. When no scripture-filled paper was found in his book, he handed it back and moved to her father. It was already known that the second slip of paper would be found in her father's songbook, and Rebecca once again reached over and squeezed Emma's knee. Bishop Weaver instructed both men to stand and accept their charge. He greeted both her father and Henry with a holy kiss and let the congregation extend their expression of sympathy and support one by one.

Katie slipped out of the room, making the excuse she needed to nurse Elizabeth, but Emma read the anguish on her face. It was evident she was on the verge of a meltdown.

Emma headed to the kitchen to help with serving, but not before Samuel held her elbow and whispered in her ear. "Daniel wants us to come over this afternoon."

Emma whispered, "I'm not sure Katie is ready for that. She's pretty upset this morning."

"Exactly why Daniel wants us to come over. He's hoping you can ease Katie's concerns."

Jacob came up behind them and stopped their conversation. "I'm calling a family meeting this afternoon and expect you both to be there."

Emma looked at Samuel and waited for him to answer. "We'll be there. What time?"

Jacob looked across the room toward Rebecca and Anna. "Three and tell your *schwesters* not to make any plans.

They waited for him to depart the room before commenting. Emma muttered, "This is not ...going to be good."

Samuel clutched her elbow tighter. "I bet not, but what else can we do but abide by his wishes ...for now at least."

"You might want to tell Daniel we can't come until later."

"I will."

Emma retreated to the kitchen just in time to hear Rebecca gloat about their father's appointment. A hush fell over the room as the women in the kitchen stopped what they were doing and stared back in disbelief. Emma pulled her *schwester* off to the side and squeezed her arm while whispering, "What are you thinking? Do you want our father's first charge to be to make you repent for your prideful manner in front of the whole congregation?"

Rebecca twisted from her grasp. "Oh, quit being so dramatic. I just said what everyone else is thinking. What harm is that?"

Emma felt heat rise to her cheeks. "You can think things all you want, but when you voice them out in the open like this, you are only causing yourself trouble."

Rebecca waved her off by making a tisk-tisk sound with her tongue.

Emma carried a stack of bowls to the front room and started to set them out across the benches turned into tables. If she and Samuel didn't push the limits with her father's new appointment, Rebecca was sure to test the waters. Out of the corner of her eye, she saw Katie and Ruth huddled in the corner of the room. Katie handed Elizabeth's diaper bag to Ruth and followed Daniel's voice across the room. The seriousness on both of their faces alarmed her, and she wondered if maybe she and Samuel should forgo visiting.

After Katie and Daniel left, Ruth carried the baby her way and stopped at her side. "Katie wasn't feeling well. Daniel's taking her home. I volunteered to watch this little one for the afternoon "

Elizabeth stretched, and Emma reached out to rub the child's belly. "I bet she'll love spending the afternoon with her *Mommi*."

Ruth flipped Elizabeth up over her shoulder and asked, "Has Katie said anything to you? Something is bothering her, but she won't open up for the life of me. I asked her again just now, and she got this far away look in her eyes and changed the subject."

Emma patted Ruth's arm, "Maybe she just needs some sleep. I bet this little one has been keeping her up at night. Nothing a long afternoon nap won't cure."

"I suppose, but I don't think so. Please promise me you'll talk to her. If anyone can figure her out, you can."

Emma smiled in Ruth's direction and went back to setting the table up for the noon-shared meal.

CHAPTER 18

At three o'clock sharp, Samuel pulled into Jacob's driveway and stopped at the front steps to let Emma out. Jacob stood on the porch. "No need to unhook your buggy. This shouldn't take long."

Emma looked over at Samuel and shrugged. "Short, and to the point, I guess."

"Okay. We don't want to give him time to start asking us too many questions. We'd never lie to him, best we keep the conversation short and sweet as well for the time being."

"I suppose so, but I hate seeing him like this. Ever since *Mamm* passed, he's been so aloof. So much different from when we were *kinner*."

"Come on, my love, give the man some grace. It's not like the last three years have been easy on him."

"*Nee*, they've not been. Having to tell me I wasn't his biological daughter and then *Mamm* dying at the same time took its toll on him."

"At least he has your older *bruder* Matthew living close by and the twins still at home. If it wasn't for them, I'm sure he'd be even more lonely and detached."

Emma snickered as he unrolled the canvas-covered door and added, "Rebecca probably still pushes his buttons, and that in itself would make anyone irritable."

"Now, now, be nice. Rebecca is your *schwester*."

She laid her finger on her chin and replied playfully, "If you want to get technical, she's not really."

"Emma Yoder, be kind."

Both were still laughing when they walked in the front door. Her father had moved to his chair at the head of the table, and Anna, Rebecca, Matthew, and his wife Sarah, looked their way as they continued to giggle.

Samuel took his hat off and nodded in Matthew's direction. Anna stood and carried a kettle to the table and poured the hot water in two waiting cups.

Emma hung her coat on the back of a chair and pulled it closer to Samuel. She was the first to speak. "So *Datt*, what do you think about your new appointment?"

He leaned back in the chair, rested his elbows on the arms, and folded his fingers together. "Challenged."

She measured a few hearty spoons of hot chocolate mix in her cup and asked, "Challenged? How so?"

Without responding to her personally, he addressed them all. "I have a few words I want to share with each of you. But before I do, let me say this. I take this charge seriously, and I expect each of you to do the same. The community will watch our every move. As a minister, I'm expected to have my house in good order."

Taking a few moments to gather his thoughts, Jacob focused first on Samuel, then Matthew. "In the eyes of the church, my house extends to the both of you as well. I anticipate you will take heed to your own households. All should follow the *Ordnung* as you promised the day you accepted membership into the church."

Matthew nodded, "I will see to it that Sarah, and I give you no reason to be concerned."

Jacob dipped his chin in his son's direction, turned toward Samuel, and asked, "And you? Can I count on you to stay true to the teachings of our forefathers?"

Samuel took in a deep breath through his nose and straightened his back before answering. "I will do my best to follow the ways of the Lord."

Emma breathed a sigh of relief. Samuel found a way to answer his question without lying, but her father was not satisfied. "That's not what I requested. I asked if your household would stay true to the *Ordnung*?"

Emma watched color make its way up under Samuel's starched white shirt, not stopping until it reached his forehead. Standing firm to his answer, he replied, "I will guide my family in the way of God's Word. If it lines up to what our forefathers held so dear, then you can rest assured we will cause you no trouble."

Her father's demeanor changed at Samuel's response. He was not pleased, but he let it pass. Without moving his glare from Samuel, he continued, "As I said, we will be watched, and I don't want any undue attention. I expect each of you to adhere to your baptismal vows."

Everyone at the table, besides Rebecca, had a solemn look. The weight of the responsibility their father would need to endure fell heavily on each of them. Rebecca however, gleamed at her father's appointment and proudly stated, "I, for one, will follow the *Ordnung* to a tee. You'll never need to worry about me."

In a harsh tone, Jacob replied, "Starting with you, Rebecca. I have one word that is meant as a warning. I've witnessed each of your weaknesses. At some point, they may cause contention in your walk with the Lord."

The snarl in her father's forehead caused Emma's stomach to flip as he uncovered six pieces of paper before him. Each of their names was printed clearly across the folded sheets. He handed Rebecca hers first. "It's totally up to you if you want to share it or keep it to yourself. Regardless, it is the one thing I see in each of you that may cause me to bring you in front of the congregation for repentance."

Rebecca boldly stood. "I have nothing to be ashamed of." She unfolded the paper and turned it around so everyone could see.

Emma read it aloud. "*Pride.*" Rebecca glared toward her father. "Pride, my word is pride? Well, I never!" she sat down in a huff.

Each of them took the sheet of paper that held their perceived fate. One by one, they read their word and sat quietly. Rebecca was the only one to share their father's warning openly.

Rebecca snarled, "Come on! I shared mine with all of you."

Emma covered her warning with her hand and said, "Unlike you Rebecca, I think each of us is taking *Datt's* warning with a bit more seriousness."

Anna, Rebecca's twin, laid her hand on Rebecca's arm and said, "I think we should pray in private about our weakness. Only then can we hope to overcome our shortcomings." Anna was the only one who could ever get a word in edgewise with Rebecca's sharp tongue.

Jacob pushed himself away from the table. "That's all I have to say for now."

No one moved from their seat, and all let out a sigh when the back door closed. Rebecca tried to take the slip of paper out of Emma's hand. "I can only imagine what you got ... I bet it was ...*perfect.*"

Emma closed her hand around the paper. Samuel reached over and patted her knee under the table before she responded, "I bet this is harder on him than we realize. If *Datt* sees something in us, it's his job to bring it to our attention."

Rebecca crossed her arms over her chest and grumbled, "Leave it to you ...know it all!"

"Leave what to me?"

"Thinking you're better than any of us."

Emma's voice cracked. "When have I ever made anyone feel like I was any better than any other member of this family?"

Matthew slapped his hand on the table. "Rebecca enough. Don't think for one minute *Datt* didn't think long and hard about what he had to share." He reached for Sarah's hand, and they stood. "For me and my family, we will be praying that God works on our flaws."

Rebecca raised and snatched the paper from Emma's grip and picked Samuel's up from the table and sneered. "Oh no, you don't. No one is leaving until I know everyone's shortcomings."

Samuel stood and grabbed Rebecca's arm, and she screeched, "Get your hands off me!"

Throwing his hands up, he stepped back just as Rebecca's mouth curved in a satisfying grin before announcing Emma's word, "*Submission.*"

She handed the sheet of paper back to Emma and said, "Well, isn't that fitting for the girl who's only half Amish. I'd say you should've run off when you had the chance. If you did, you wouldn't have to worry about submitting to anyone but yourself."

Anna covered her mouth and gasped, "Rebecca, please stop." She turned to Emma and continued, "Don't listen to a word she says. She doesn't mean it."

Rebecca spewed out her words as if the devil himself possessed her. "She should have stayed in Sugarcreek with her other family."

Without giving anyone a chance to recover from her outburst, Rebecca unfolded Samuel's paper and smirked before saying, "*Loyalty.*"

Emma picked the paper off the floor and faced Rebecca, eye to eye. "I will take my word to the only one who can help me overcome it, and I propose you do the same."

Matthew shook his head and pulled Sarah toward the door, "You keep this up, and you'll be the first one bowing a knee in front of the church."

Samuel seized the note from Rebecca's fingers and then held out Emma's coat while she slipped her arms in the sleeves, as he warned, "Rebecca, I'd hold your tongue if I were you."

She waved him off and growled, "You made your choice, now deal with it!"

Emma stepped in front of Samuel when he opened the door and asked, "What did she mean by that?"

He glanced back over his shoulder before shutting the door. "I've long given up trying to figure that one out."

Emma pulled the wool blanket up over her lap as soon as she crawled inside their buggy. She waited for Samuel to check on Oliver's harness before joining her inside. Once he did, she asked, "Rebecca acted like you should know what she's talking about."

"Oh ...I have an idea."

"You do? What's that?"

Samuel tightened Oliver's reins for him to move away from the hitching post. "When you were in Sugarcreek a few years ago, she tried to stir up trouble between us, which I put a stop to quickly."

Emma sighed, "Every time I think she's gotten over whatever it is that eats away at her about me, it pops back up when I least expect it."

He molded his hand around hers. "Rebecca is the least of our worries. I think we need to tell Daniel about your *datt's* warning. Not sure why he pointed out loyalty to me. Unless he already knows more than he's letting on."

Emma cupped her free hand over his and said, "Oh Samuel, I bet Henry Mast from Pinecraft said something to Sarah's father."

"I'm not sure about that. Henry acted like he and his brother didn't speak often. And besides, Henry's New Order believes as we do now. Why would he purposely stir up trouble for us?"

Emma twisted toward him. "But you know the Amish grapevine, it spreads like wildfire, no matter where it starts."

"We need to keep our bible studying to ourselves for now. I'm half inclined to put a stop to Daniel coming over as well. The way your father questioned me makes me think he already knows something. Let's let the dust settle for the time being."

Emma moved closer and laid her head on his shoulder. "I'm sorry I haven't always been totally submissive to you."

Samuel kissed the top of her *kapp*. "Listen to me, I knew way back when we were catching tadpoles in the creek, you had a mind of your own. If I wanted something else in a wife, I had plenty of time to look elsewhere. Now, I'm not giving you a pass on the whole thing about tramping off to Pinecraft without me, but looking back, it was all for a good reason. If you hadn't gone, we wouldn't have met Alvin and Lynette, and we surely wouldn't have found Jesus."

She wrapped her hand around his arm. "But I think we would have, because you and Daniel were already questioning things. I can't imagine you not finding a way to eventually share that with me."

"I suppose you're right. It wouldn't have been something I could have kept from you forever."

Samuel pulled up to the front porch and secured the reins as Emma asked, "How can the ministers expect us to do as they say if it's not what the bible instructs?"

Samuel shifted toward her. "There are many discrepancies between the bible and what we were taught. But we can only go by what we read is true. Look at Henry Mast, he found the truth, and it forced him to leave his Old Order community to seek fellowship elsewhere."

Emma added, "And look at Alvin's parents; they did the same thing. They left and joined a Mennonite Church. Will we have to do that?"

"I wish I had an answer, but for right now, we'll keep seeking the truth and let God reveal to us what door he'll open and which he'll close. When we walk in faith, he will guide our way. I'm confident of that, for sure."

"I'm scared."

He pulled her close. "No reason to be fearful. We can only control the choices we make at this very moment. God had it all planned out, even before we took our first breath."

She looked into his eyes and asked, "He even knew James wasn't meant to be with us, didn't He?"

"He did, just like He knows when he'll send us another. And He will provide us more when the time is right, even if it means we have to use some of Dr. Smithson's natural prevention recommendations."

Emma's cheeks took on a rosy hue and asked, "Do you think God is preventing us from having more *kinner* right now because He wants us to be free to work for Him?"

Samuel lifted her chin and warmed her chilled lips before saying, "I believe that's exactly what He's doing. But his calling is not only to salvation; it's also to a life of serving him and our fellow believers."

Samuel reached under his seat and brought out a small black bible. "Let me show you what I found last night." He flipped the pages until he stopped on the scripture he had highlighted in yellow, and read it aloud, "*Go into all the world and preach the gospel to all creation.*"

Emma laid her hand on the page. "He's calling us to share what we're learning with our community, isn't he?"

Samuel shut the book and tucked it back under his seat. "He is, and how can we deny that. I feel so strongly about our calling; I can't think of anything else."

"Is this the battle you spoke about?"

"It is. Like Alvin told us, challenging our Old Order ways will cause great division in this community, and we must be prepared for what is to come. All we need to do is plant the seed and then get out of God's way. He'll do the rest."

Emma smiled before saying, "I take my comment about being scared back. I'm not scared; I'm excited to see what God will do in this community and with us. The more we talk about it, the more I believe James was just a stepping-stone for God to use us for His greater mission. Marie told me once that I needed to be a woman who says *yes* to God. I want to be that woman."

Samuel pulled her back into his embrace. "And I want to be a man of God who leads his family to the Lord according to all of His Word, not just selected bits and pieces."

***

Daniel sat on the edge of the bed and rested his elbows on his knees. "Katie, I don't know what else to say. I've apologized a dozen times for keeping this from you. But I had to make a choice, and I chose to marry you, even when I knew the church was not teaching you everything."

Katie rested her arm over her eyes, trying to ease the pounding in her head. "But you lied to God and to me."

"I didn't lie to God. He knew my heart."

"But a lie is a lie, and a sin is a sin, regardless of how you rationalize it in your head."

Daniel sat up straight and moved her arm away from her face. "Then tell me. If I had told you what the ministers were teaching was not the whole truth, would you have left your family and friends for me?"

Katie turned her face to him. "You know the answer to that. I was already baptized. I would have had no other choice but to let you go."

"Exactly, you would have chosen the Amish church over me."

She rolled off the bed and walked to the window. "This is all too much. I don't even know how I feel about any of it. Why would they steer us wrong? They are men of God, put in charge of nurturing our spiritual lives. I can't believe Bishop Weaver would do anything that didn't line up with God."

Daniel walked to her. "I'm not trying to turn you against the leaders of the church, I'm not, I promise. But as the head of this family, I want you and Elizabeth to know the whole truth, not just selected verses."

Katie wiped her chin with the back of her hand. "Bishop Weaver and the ministers are good teachers. They share God's Word with us all the time."

"They do, but they don't teach us everything. I don't want to be a bits and pieces Christian; I want to be an all-in follower of Jesus."

"See what I mean? You call yourself a Christian, not Amish."

Daniel picked up her hands. "Because I am a Christian — an Amish Christian."

She pulled her hands from his, "We're going to be shunned, I know it."

He placed his hands on her shoulders and turned her back to face him. "Jesus never said following Him would be easy, and even if it comes down to that, I know without a doubt it will be worth it."

She twisted from his grasp. "How can you say that? My parents will be forbidden to talk to us or sit at our table. I can't do it. I won't take that kind of chance. Please, Daniel, you must get rid of your English bible before someone finds out. It will be the death of our family, for sure and certain."

Daniel turned toward the window and stood silent.

Katie pleaded, "Please don't do this to us. I can't ask you to stop believing, but you must keep those thoughts to yourself. You must stop studying with Samuel and Emma. If Jacob gets word of it, he'll have to bring his own daughter in front of the church, and that would be heart-wrenching."

Without looking in her direction, he muttered, "I'll stop meeting with Samuel and Emma if that's what you want."

"And the bible? You'll dispose of it?"

He didn't say a word but continued to stare out the window.

She walked over to him and touched his arm. "What about your bible?"

His stance hardened, and the muscles in his jaw twitched at her question. When he refused to answer, she turned and ran downstairs.

Her bare feet against the stairs reaffirmed her frustration, but he couldn't make a promise he couldn't keep. Refraining from spending time at Samuel's was one thing, but getting rid of his bible; that was asking too much.

***

Katie curled up in a rocking chair and wrapped a blanket around her shoulders. A few lingering rays of sunshine spilled through the window as they made their way closer to the horizon. Smoke swirled from her parent's roof as she watched her father walk to the barn. She couldn't help but wonder if he knew of what Daniel spoke of. Salvation through Christ, how was that even possible?

She saw both her father and mother as faithful followers of the *Ordnung*. They had a happy life, full of friends and family, along with sharing the burden of their fellow church members without complaint. Not once in her life had she heard either of them complain or wonder what life would be outside of their faith? If it worked for them, why would Daniel think it couldn't work for them as well?

When the blanket slipped from her shoulder; she bound it tighter and pulled her knees up to her chest. There was a stillness in the room that made the pulsation over her eyes feel like boulders. Laying her head in her folded arms over her knees, she saw no way out of the inevitable doom lingering over them. She had to stop it, but how?

With her eyes still closed and her head buried, she heard Daniel's footsteps stopping near her. "I'll do anything for you, you know that, but I won't stop reading."

Without lifting her head, she willed herself to keep quiet. She wanted to lash out, but her spirit held back in submission. A surge of cold air swirled around her chair when he opened the door. After the squeak of the hinges quelled, she opened her eyes and followed him across the yard and into the barn. Her heart cried out to him, even in her pain.

***

Daniel filled each grain bucket and broke the ice free from the troughs before retreating to the tack room at the back of the barn. His Sunday church clothes prevented him from doing anything but contemplate what Katie was asking of him. Perhaps once she calmed down, he could reason with her. They had only been married a little over a year, but it was long enough to know he wasn't wrong in putting God first. That was the one thing his Amish community did right. They put God first, then family, and then community. How could she be asking him to put her first?

"Daniel, are you in here?" Samuel hollered.

Daniel followed Samuel's voice. "*Jah*."

"I saw your footprints headed this way. Emma went up to the house."

"Not sure Katie's up for company, but if anyone can get through to her, it's Emma."

"How did it go at Jacob's?"

"Let's just say he gave us all a warning."

"A warning?"

"*Jah*, a warning to let us know he will be watching us, and he won't think twice about bringing us in front of the church to repent if he sees us stepping outside the *Ordnung*."

"You have Jacob; I have Katie. I promised her I wouldn't be studying with you and Emma anymore. She's terrified of being shunned."

Samuel gripped his best friend's shoulder and tapped his chest with his other hand. "For now, we can honor their wishes, but it won't stop what we already know in here."

"I agree, and in time I pray the Lord will help me find a way to get Katie to feel it too."

Samuel added, "Remember you can't be her Holy Spirit. Only God can put that desire in her heart. The way I see it, she's fighting it because her spirit is already trying to convict her."

Daniel leaned back on the workbench. "Man I hope you're right."

***

Emma stepped inside the kitchen and pushed the basement door shut as she entered, calling out, "Katie?"

When Katie didn't answer, she removed her coat and boots and called her name through the house. Back in the kitchen, she tilted her head, turning an ear to a muffled cry. She opened the basement door and listened. In the distance, she heard Katie moan, "I won't let him do it," and then the sound of ripping paper, "I won't let him shame us," and more tearing of paper.

Emma followed her voice to the back of the basement near the coal furnace. There, on her knees, in front of the open furnace door, Katie ripped page after page of Daniel's bible and tossed it in the fire.

Emma dropped to the floor and grabbed the half-torn book from her hands. "What are you doing?"

Katie tugged it back. "I won't let him take me away from my family. Elizabeth needs to know her grandparents."

Emma lowered her voice. "You're not thinking clearly Daniel would never do that."

"But he would, and he has. He is going against the rules he agreed to when he became a member of the church. If the leaders find out, they'll shun us. I'll be forced to choose between him and the church."

Emma shut the glass door of the furnace and took the leather-bound book from her hands. "Daniel only wants you to know the truth."

In a frenzied manner, Katie scooped a few loose pages off the floor and held them tight to her chest and turned back to the fire. Emma grabbed her arm and pulled her away. "Stop, you're not thinking this through. Burning his bible isn't going to do anything. He already knows what is written. You can't burn it from his heart."

Katie recoiled from her grip. "I'm so sick of hearing about all this truth you're all talking about. The only truth I need to hear is Daniel giving up this silly notion and staying true to the promises he made to both me and God."

Emma flipped to the back of the bible to Ephesians and followed her finger until it stopped on Chapter 2, where verses eight and nine were underlined in red ink. "Read this." She handed Katie the tattered book.

Katie pushed Emma's hand away. "I don't need to, I already have. He had that page marked."

"Then you know the truth. Why would you still want to burn it?"

"Our marriage is built on nothing but lies."

Emma sat on the floor in front of her and took both of her hands. "Your marriage was built on love, not lies, and you can't really believe that."

"But Emma, you don't understand. He never intended to follow the *Ordnung*. And he married me knowing he couldn't agree with what was being taught. Daniel lied, and I can't forgive that."

"Katie, listen to yourself. You're condemning Daniel for lying, but you're committing a sin just as great as his by not forgiving him. How can one sin be any less than the other?"

"Oh, Emma, what are we going to do?"

Emma stood and reached out her hand to help her up off the floor, "To begin with, we're both going to trust in the Lord and then trust in our husbands. God gave them the authority over us, and we have to leave any decision like this up to them."

"But if we do, we may be excommunicated."

"I can't say that might not happen. But if I didn't learn anything else from my time spent in Florida, I learned we can only concern ourselves with this very moment. Once I realized I have no control over anything that might or might not happen, it was like a huge weight was lifted from my shoulders."

Katie took a tissue from her pocket and wiped her eyes. "I'm so confused," she pointed to the book Emma held. "Are there other things in there that were kept from us?"

"I'm sure of it, but we're only going to discover more if we study it for ourselves."

"But Emma."

"But nothing, this is much bigger than either of us can fathom. You don't think the Lord orchestrated this to happen? He wants our community to understand the truth of Jesus and not just a bunch of rules and regulations created by man. I agree we need to stand in unity and keep ourselves separated from the outside world. That's what keeps us focused on God, and I wouldn't want it any other way. But I also realize we can continue to live a simple life, serving the Lord and loving our neighbors all while sharing the truth in why Jesus died for us."

Katie sniffled. "But we aren't supposed to evangelize; it goes against everything we believe in."

Emma picked up the bible and held it out to her. "Show me in here where it says that, and I'll show you where Jesus instructs us to go out and spread his name to the world."

"What? We're told to talk to people about Jesus."

"We are, and He may have appointed Samuel, Daniel, and even you and me to be His messengers. And how can we say no to God?"

Emma wrapped her arms around her middle, and Katie rested her head on her shoulder and whispered, "I don't want to."

"And neither do I. I know how hard this must be for you and it is for me too. But we must let our husbands lead their families the way they see fit, even if it means it goes against our Old Order ways."

"But Emma, do you understand what this means for us? We will be forced to live as strangers to our family."

"It might very well mean that, but we'll always have each other. And who knows? It may be the special gift God gave us to serve Him."

"A special gift?"

"Yes, God gives each of us spiritual gifts that we are to use to better the Kingdom of God."

"How do you know that?"

Emma took the tattered book from her hand and said, "Here, let me show you where He teaches us about our spiritual gifts."

EPILOGUE

Wrapping herself tightly with her cream-colored shawl, Emma walked the fifteen minutes to the cemetery.

"My sweet boy, it's been six months since I visited you here at your graveside. I still cringe when I think about your tiny body lying in this cold earth. But I've learned so much since I held your lifeless body in my arms. I've learned that healing can come in many forms from many other people. Healing doesn't mean I've stopped feeling sad or miss what could have been if you had lived. No, it means by losing you, I gained so much more. It turns out in the depths of despair, and in the wake of loss, it isn't the end, but just the beginning.

So many times, I have thanked God for allowing me the time I felt you grow inside of me. But more than that, I thank Him for finally showing me that your precious soul is in heaven for eternity, and I will see you again. Don't get me wrong, we lost a lot when we lost you, and I hope and pray your *datt* and I will never have to endure such loss again. But the bittersweet reality is, we have grown so much through this journey.

I don't know if the hole in our hearts will ever close, but I do know that we have more of Jesus in there than we ever had before. All because God chose to carry you into eternity. Had you not been taken from us; we would have never found the truth in Jesus. I will always find comfort in that. I've finally found peace, and I'm ready to move on. I'm a vastly different person from the one who carried your tiny body under my heart for seven months.

God never promised us an easy passage, but he does promise to always walk beside us. You'd be so proud of your *datt*. He's been called into service for the Lord, and he has taken his charge with honor. I'm not sure what will happen once we step out in faith to our community, but we both trust the Lord to pave our path. Your *datt* and I have made a promise to God to share the word of salvation through Jesus. We won't stop until we have shared His promises with as many people as we can.

I read somewhere that it's not how we get to heaven but how many people we take with us that matters most. My relationship with heaven has always been a strange, hopeful plea, that Lord willing, I will be good enough to walk through those pearly gates. But because of you, I can rest assured my name is written in His book, right beside yours. Heaven is a place I think about every day and a place I want to be.

Right here beside you lies my *Mamm*, and I'm so comforted she is there with you.

Mamm, you have no idea what your note has done for me. It took me months to truly understand what your words meant, but they saved my life. One of the biggest things I've learned over the past six months was that God wants to share both in our joys and our sorrows. He wants us to be content in trusting His plans, and He wants others to see Christ in us. Even though I never saw that in you while you were alive, I am so honored your last words to me were those that helped me search for the truth. Without knowing I had a God who wanted a personal relationship with me centered around love and not works, it was a miracle. Because of your note, a burden was lifted that literally saved me from drowning in the depths of despair.

So, until we meet again, I will be faithful in the wait and know there is more to life on the other side waiting for me. See you both soon."

Read more from ...

The Amish Women of Lawrence County Series
Rebecca's Amish Heart Restored

Rebecca's

Amish Heart Restored

THE AMISH WOMEN OF
LAWRENCE COUNTY SERIES - BOOK 2

Tracy Fredrychowski

327

PROLOGUE – BOOK 2
April - Willow Springs, Pennsylvania

The rhythmic movement of Rebecca Byler's spinning wheel picked up speed as she thought about her run-in with her younger *schwester*, Emma. In all her twenty-three years, she'd never been more aggravated than she was at that moment. When the roving of alpaca fiber she let slide through her thumb and index finger hit a clump of dark matter, she pulled back and let the draft of yarn fall to the floor. "Ugh! I don't have time for this."

Rebecca's twin, Anna, stopped the drum roller and turned her way. "Now what?"

"I'm still finding bits of hay in the roving. You're not getting it clean enough."

Anna stooped down and picked up the tan cloud of fiber and held it toward the light of the window. "I don't see anything."

"I felt it. Look closer."

Anna held it out. "I don't see a thing, show me."

Rebecca waved her off. "Just be more careful when you're picking and carding it. We can't afford to have our customers complain our yarn isn't clean enough."

Anna threw the clump back in the carding box and asked, "What's got you all worked up today?"

Irritation crept up Rebecca's neck as she replayed the argument, she had at the bakery earlier that morning. "Can you believe Emma had the nerve to tell me I was hateful?"

"Why did she say that?"

"Thing's would be so much better around here if she would've stayed in Sugarcreek."

Anna tilted her head. "I bet you provoked her. It doesn't sound like something Emma would say."

Rebecca snarled, "Why do you always insist on taking her side?"

"I'm not taking anyone's side, but I know how you get."

"And what's that supposed to mean?"

"You tell me. You've been harping on Emma for months and nit-picking about every little thing. If you don't watch it, word's going to get back to *datt,* and then you'll really have something to fuss about."

"Me? It's Emma who should be worried. I don't know what she and Samuel are up to, but they've got something they're hiding, and I'll figure it out one way or another."

"Rebecca, why are you so set on causing them trouble?"

"She's the one who thinks she's better than everyone else."

"How do you figure?"

"Think about it. First, she runs off to Sugarcreek to spend time with her birth family and leaves *Mamm* when she needed her most. In my books, *Mamm* would still be alive if she hadn't spent the last few months of her life worrying about Emma. Next, she strings Samuel along for months only to come back assuming he'd drop everything and take her back."

Anna laid a cloud of fiber in front of the teeth of the drum. She turned the handle to feed the batt through, combing it in long smooth batches. "Why are you harping on this? That was three years ago."

"Because it was the start of her prancing around like we owed her something."

"Come on, Rebecca, you're exaggerating. Emma doesn't act like that at all. You don't give her enough credit. How do you think you would have felt if you found out *Mamm* and *Datt* weren't really your parents after sixteen years?"

"Elated that Emma wasn't really my *schwester*!"

Anna gasped, "You take that back. You don't really mean that."

"I won't, and I do."

"You are hateful, and I can see why Emma said that to you. You best take your attitude to the Lord before it gets you in trouble."

The bell above the door to their father's shop jingled, and Rebecca snapped, "I'll get that."

Their father had built a room off the side of his furniture shop to sell the yarn they produced from the alpacas they raised on their farm. A divider kept the washing, sorting, and spinning area separate from the display floor and the customers. In the two years since they opened, *Stitch-n'-Time,* their alpaca and specialty wool yarns had become a popular stop for both the Amish and English. They even started offering hand-made products, on consignment, from the women in their community.

Rebecca made her way around two spinning wheels and pulled the curtain aside to step out in the store. Along the outside wall, their father had built display racks to hold the hand-dyed fiber. An array of baskets sat on the worktable in the middle of the room that contained mittens, hats, socks, and scarves available for sale. Canisters of different sized crochet hooks and knitting needles adorned the counter by the cash register.

It didn't take her but a second to recognize Samuel's broad shoulders and wisps of dark curls that flipped up at the back of his straw hat. "Samuel?"

He turned toward her voice. "Rebecca, I'd like a word with you."

"Okay, what about?"

"Let's step outside."

Her lip turned upward before saying, "The porch? Not so sure that would be the honorable thing to do with your wife's *schwester*."

"I'm in no mood for your shenanigans," he moved her way and whispered, "I can air your dirty laundry right here so Anna and your *datt* can hear, or we can take this outside."

She moved to the door and to the far end of the porch. "So, what is so important that we had to come out here?"

"We can start with your visit to the bakery this morning. Don't you think Emma's had enough to deal with the last six months? She doesn't need your verbal abuse to add to it."

She crossed her arms over her chest. "I only spoke the truth."

"I don't believe a word that comes from your mouth. It wouldn't be the first time you've stirred up trouble for your own benefit."

She snapped her head in his direction. "Like I've said before, if you bring any of that back up, I'll tell your sweet little Emma exactly how her wonder boy behaved while she was away."

He moved closer and snarled, "Don't threaten me."

She backed up. "*Ohhh* ...did I hit a nerve?"

"Don't think for a minute I'll stand by and watch you harass my wife. Whatever you think she's done is no concern of yours, and I'll warn you one last time. Keep your snide remarks and accusations to yourself."

"Or what? You'll tell who, the bishop?"

"I mean it, Rebecca, don't go there."

Rebecca walked back to the door and held her hand on the knob, and said, "The way I see it, you have a lot more to lose than I do."

He walked toward her, stopped at her shoulder, and muttered in her ear. "That's where you're wrong. I've already made my peace with God ...have you?"

She snapped back. "But have you made your peace with my *schwester*?"

He didn't respond to her question but walked off the porch and into his waiting buggy.

Her nails dug into the palm of her hand, and she clenched her teeth at his comment. For three years, she'd kept his secret, holding onto it until just the right time when it could cause the most pain. If he thought for one minute, she wouldn't use it to rage her revenge, then he was sadly mistaken. If she planned it right, her little *schwester* would be sorry she ever stepped foot back in Willow Springs.

Read more of Rebecca's story in the second book of
The Amish Women of Lawrence County Series
Rebecca's Amish Heart Restored

APPENDIX

Ginger Snap Cookies

Ingredients:

3/4 cup shortening

1 cup granulated sugar

1 egg

1/4 cup molasses

1 cup all-purpose flour

1 cup wheat flour

1/4 teaspoon salt

2 teaspoons baking soda

1 teaspoon ground cinnamon

1/2 teaspoon ground cloves

1 tablespoon ground ginger

Additional 1/2 cup sugar for dipping

Instructions:

- Preheat oven to 350°. Lightly grease cookie sheets.
- With a mixer, cream shortening and sugar until well blended. Add egg and molasses until combined.
- Mix flour, salt, baking soda, cinnamon, cloves, and ginger together in a separate bowl.

- Gradually add the dry ingredients to the mixing bowl at low speed until everything is incorporated and a dough forms.

- Using a small melon ball scoop, drop dough on prepared cookie sheets.

- Dip a glass bottom in sugar and lightly press each dough ball down.

- Bake for 8-10 minutes.

- Allow them to cool on a cookie sheet for a few minutes, then transfer to a cooling rack to cool completely.

WHAT DID YOU THINK?

First of all, thank you for purchasing The Amish Women of Lawrence County - Emma. I hope you will enjoy all the books in this series.

You could have picked any number of books to read, but you chose this book, and for that, I am incredibly grateful. I hope it added value and quality to your everyday life. If so, it would be nice to share this book with your friends and family on social media.

If you enjoyed this book and found some benefit in reading it, I'd like to hear from you and hope that you could take some time to post a review on Amazon. Your feedback and support will help me improve my writing craft for future projects.

If you loved visiting Willow Springs, I invite you to sign up for my private email list, where you'll get to explore more of the characters of this Old-Order Amish Community.

Sign up at https://dl.bookfunnel.com/v9wmnj7kve and download the novella that starts this series, *The Amish Women of Lawrence County*.

GLOSSARY

Pennsylvania Dutch "Deutsch" Words

Ausbund. Amish songbook.

bruder. Brother

datt. Father or dad.

denki. "Thank You."

doddi. Grandfather.

doddi haus. A small house usually next to or attached to the main house.

jah. "Yes."

kapp. Covering or prayer cap.

kinner. Children.

mamm. Mother or mom.

mommi. Grandmother.

nee. "No."

Ordnung. Order or set of rules the Amish follow.

schwester. Sister.

singeon. Singing/youth gathering.

The Amish are a religious group typically referred to as Pennsylvania Dutch, Pennsylvania Germans, or Pennsylvania

Deutsch. They are descendants of early German immigrants to Pennsylvania, and their beliefs center around living a conservative lifestyle. They arrived between the late 1600s and the early 1800s to escape religious persecutions in Europe. They first settled in Pennsylvania with the promise of religious freedom by William Penn. Most Pennsylvania Dutch still speak a variation of their original German language as well as English.

ABOUT THE AUTHOR

Tracy Fredrychowski lives a life similar to the stories she writes. Striving to simplify her life, she often shares her simple living tips and ideas on her website and blog at https://tracyfredrychowski.com.

Growing up in rural northwestern Pennsylvania, country living was instilled in her from an early age. As a young woman, she was traumatized by the murder of a young Amish woman in her rural Pennsylvania community. She became dedicated to sharing stories of their simple existence. She inspires her readers to live God-centered lives through faith, family, and community. If you want to enjoy more of the Amish of Lawrence County, she invites you to join her on Facebook. There she shares her friend Jim Fisher's Amish photography, recipes, short stories, and an inside look at her favorite Amish community nestled in northwestern Pennsylvania, deep in Amish Country.

Instagram.com/tracyfredrychowski/

Facebook.com/tracyfredrychowskiauthor/

Facebook.com/groups/tracyfredrychowski/

Made in United States
Troutdale, OR
11/20/2023

14758960R00215